DEADLY RITUAL

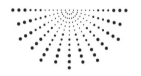

D. S. BUTLER

Deadly Obsession
Deadly Motive
Deadly Revenge
Deadly Justice
Deadly Ritual
Deadly Payback
Deadly Game
Lost Child
Her Missing Daughter
Bring Them Home
Where Secrets Lie

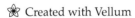 Created with Vellum

DEADLY RITUAL is the fifth book in the DS Jack Mackinnon Crime Series.

Jack is back and this time it's deadly...

The police believe they have uncovered a ritualistic voodoo murder when they find a wooden disc in the mouth of a murder victim. When another victim is discovered, it's up to DS Mackinnon and the team to find the killer before anymore blood is shed.

DEADLY RITUAL is a British police procedural, perfect for fans of Peter James and his Roy Grace detective series.

CHAPTER ONE

A FRANTIC STREAM OF BUBBLES escaped from Alfie's mouth. He was trying his best to keep his mouth shut, but how much longer could he hold his breath?

He struggled desperately, even though he knew it was no use. He fought against the hands that held him, fighting to get fresh air into his burning lungs.

His bony knees knocked against the cold enamel of the bath. He pushed his hands flat against the cold surface, trying to lever himself up. If he could just raise his head a little bit, break the surface of the water, he could take a breath.

But the grip around his throat grew tighter, and the hands above him thrust him back down viciously. His head slammed against the side of the bath.

Alfie's wide staring eyes looked up, and through the trail of bubbles, he could see the tall figures of his aunt and his uncle looming above him.

Now there was a high-pitched buzzing in his ears. He couldn't hold his breath much longer.

Just as he started to see little dots dancing in front of his eyes and darkness closing in on him, narrowing his vision, he felt the hands around his throat release their grip.

Alfie's face broke the surface of the water. He gasped for breath, and his legs slid against the slippery surface of the bath as he tried to push himself away from his aunt and uncle.

"I think he's had enough," Alfie's aunt said. "The spirit has gone. I can see it in his eyes."

Alfie's terrified gaze focused on his uncle. The fat man sat on the side of the bath, his grey trousers damp from Alfie's splashes.

He cocked his head to one side. "Has it gone, Alfie?"

Alfie nodded frantically. He grabbed his knees to his skinny chest as coughs racked his body. He wanted to say the devil had gone. He wanted to tell them he would be good now. But he couldn't get the words out.

After what seemed like an eternity, Alfie's uncle stood up and nodded once to Alfie's aunt. Then he turned and walked out of the bathroom.

Alfie rested his forehead on his knees. He wanted to get out of the bath and out of this bathroom as quickly as possible, but his arms and legs were shaking. He was panting for breath.

Alfie's aunt jutted out her chin. "You'll be a good boy now, won't you, Alfie?"

"Yes," Alfie said. His voice was hoarse from coughing. "I promise."

His aunt reached out and grabbed a faded green towel that had seen better days. She held it out to him, and Alfie gripped the side of the bath as he pulled himself up.

The first time it had happened, he'd been shy, not wanting his aunt to see him naked. But after the first time, he knew being seen naked was the least of his worries.

Alfie took the towel from her outstretched hand and pressed the rough cotton to his cheek, smothering a sob.

His hands were still shaking as he clambered over the side of the bath.

"Will this be the last time, Alfie?"

Alfie nodded, looking down at the wet footprints on the bath mat. "Yes, Aunt Erika."

"The spirit has gone? Are you sure?"

She grabbed Alfie. Her hands grasped Alfie's face, one on each cheek, pinching him. She put her head close to his. He could smell the coffee on her breath as her fierce eyes searched his face.

"I hope so, Alfie. I really do," she said.

"I promise," Alfie said, trying to pull his face away from her pinching fingers.

She nodded. "That's good, Alfie. Otherwise…" Her dark eyes locked on his. "Otherwise I'll have no choice but to involve Mr. X."

Alfie felt bile rise in his throat. It wasn't the first time his aunt had mentioned Mr. X.

CHAPTER TWO

WHEN THE SCHOOL BELL RANG, Alfie felt his heart plummet. Other kids looked forward to the end of school, but Alfie didn't. Not since his grandmother had left him in the care of his aunt and uncle.

After Alfie had gotten into a fight, sticking up for his younger brother, Mickey, his grandmother had flung up her hands and said she was sick of Alfie's behaviour. Did she have the energy to run around after Alfie and his brother she had asked him, wagging a finger in his face.

Alfie had opened his mouth to try to explain that the fight hadn't been his fault, but she'd snapped at him not to talk back. She had rolled her eyes and looked up at the ceiling and said, "I'm too old for this. I never asked for you and your brother. I don't have the energy to look after children, especially ones as bad as you."

She'd been saying that for as long as Alfie could remember, so Alfie didn't take it seriously. Not until six months

4

ago when his grandmother announced that he would be living with his aunt and uncle from then on.

At the time, Alfie wasn't too upset. In fact, he thought it might be fun.

He was wrong.

He'd never expected to miss his grandmother, but he did. He missed the fact she'd cooked him dinner every night. He missed her nagging him to clean his teeth before he went to bed. He missed how she insisted he say his prayers. He even missed her nagging him for playing on the Xbox too much. But most of all, he missed feeling safe.

Alfie heard a voice call out to him from across the classroom.

"All right, Alfie," Francis Eze said as he swaggered over to Alfie's desk. Francis had already taken off his school tie and stuffed it in the pocket of his trousers. "You fancy going boarding?"

Alfie stuffed his school books in his bag and shrugged. He wanted to go. He'd always loved skateboarding, but his aunt had thrown Alfie's skateboard away. She said there wasn't room for things like that in the flat.

"You can have a go on mine," Francis said.

Alfie glanced up at the clock on the wall. Three-thirty. He was supposed to go straight back to the flat after school. His aunt didn't finish work until five-thirty, but somehow she always knew when he didn't come straight home. Alfie thought she must have spies watching out for him in the block of flats.

But Alfie didn't want to go back to the flat. He didn't want to sit there for three hours, worrying that his aunt and uncle might decide he needed to be cleansed of spirits again.

"C'mon, Alfie. It's my new board. You'll love it. I haven't had a chance to try it out yet."

Alfie had heard a lot about Francis's new skateboard. He tried not to be jealous, but it was hard when it was all Francis had talked about for the last two days.

"It's really awesome and it's got a skull and crossbones between the wheels."

Alfie lifted his school bag onto his shoulder. He hadn't gone boarding for ages.

"All right then."

Francis grinned. "You can have the first go, if you like."

They grabbed the board from Francis's locker and headed outside.

As soon as they'd rounded the corner and were out of sight of the school, Francis pulled a packet of cigarettes from his pocket. He offered one to Alfie who shook his head.

"Suit yourself," Francis said. He stopped beside a low brick wall and set the skateboard down on the floor so he could light up. He took a shallow drag on the cigarette. Francis smoked more for show than habit.

Alfie kept his distance. He didn't want his aunt and uncle smelling smoke on him when he got home.

"Where do you want to go?" Francis asked.

Alfie picked up the skateboard and looked admiringly at the smooth paintwork. It was black with a bolt of lightning running down the centre. He turned the board over and saw the skull and crossbones Francis had been so keen on.

The empty black eyes of the skull stared out at him. Alfie shivered and put the skateboard back on the floor.

"What about the steps near your place?"

The steps by Victoria House on the Towers Estate were fantastic for boarding.

They could do some jumps there. Alfie felt a little thrill as he imagined the sensation he got in the pit of his stomach when he launched himself for a jump.

Alfie wished he still had his board. He loved skateboarding. It was the one thing he'd always been good at.

He wasn't too good at schoolwork. He used to get into trouble for talking too much. He was uncoordinated and rubbish at most sports, but skateboarding was different. On a skateboard, he could almost fly.

Francis looked wary. "Jumps?" He looked down at his new skateboard. "I dunno. That's for kids."

Francis only said that because he wasn't as good as Alfie. He was too nervous, always worrying about falling.

Alfie kicked at an old Coke can someone had chucked away. "You're scared," he said.

"I am not," Francis said. "I…" Suddenly, Francis's eyes widened.

He threw the cigarette on the ground and stamped on it, frantically fanning the air.

Alfie turned to see Mr. Xander, Head of Sport, and the scariest teacher at their school, walking towards them.

He was a tall black man, with huge broad shoulders and a very sour face. Alfie didn't think he'd ever seen Mr. Xander smile.

"I hope I didn't see you with a cigarette, boy," Mr.

Xander said. His low, gravelly voice made goose bumps appear on Alfie's arms.

Francis looked around as though he thought Mr. Xander must be talking to somebody else.

He raised his open palms and said, "No, Mr. Xander, I didn't have a cigarette, did I, Alfie? I don't smoke."

Mr. Xander looked at them for a moment with narrowed eyes, and Alfie felt his stomach twist. The last thing he needed was Mr. Xander to send a letter home to his aunt and uncle about smoking.

"Honest, sir," Francis said. "It wasn't us."

"There's one thing I hate more than an obnoxious snivelling twelve-year-old, Francis. Do you know what that is?" The big man stood over them and put a huge hand on Francis's shoulder.

Francis shook his head. "Um…No, sir,"

"A liar," Mr. Xander said.

Just as Alfie thought they would definitely be in for a detention at the very least, Mr. Xander swivelled on his heel and stalked off back in the direction of the school.

When the teacher was out of earshot, Francis gave out a low whistle. "That was close."

"You were asking for trouble," Alfie said. "He lives just around the corner. You should have waited until we were further away."

Francis shot Alfie a scornful look. "Don't be such a baby. I can't believe you're scared of Mr. Xander."

Alfie leaned down to pick up the skateboard. "Get a move on," he said. "Or we won't have any time to board."

"Of course, I knew Mr. Xander wouldn't actually do

anything. I mean he can't when we are not in school," Francis said, suddenly full of bravado, as they walked to the Towers Estate.

Alfie smirked. Francis was such an idiot sometimes.

For the next hour, Alfie was in heaven as he spun and glided over the square by Victoria House.

When Alfie leaped from the top step, he bent his knees, feeling the board beneath him and for a fraction of a second he felt weightless. He landed with a clatter, but managed to stay upright.

He picked up the skateboard and turned back to Francis. "Your turn."

Francis reluctantly took the board and slowly climbed the steps. At the top, he looked down at Alfie, then took a deep breath. He propelled himself along, the wheels rattling against the concrete.

But just before the jump, Francis wimped out and jumped off. The board rolled down the steps on its own, landing upside down with its wheels still spinning.

"What happened?" Alfie said, picking up the skateboard.

"I don't want to do jumps," Francis said. He sat down on the top step. "It's my board and you're hogging it."

Alfie climbed the steps and sat beside him. "Sorry," he said.

Francis shrugged. "Why don't you buy another board? You could keep it at my house if you like. Your aunt and uncle would never know."

"No money."

Francis pushed at the skateboard with the tip of his shoe. "Well, you can use mine anytime you like."

"Thanks."

Alfie looked across the square at a group of younger kids kicking about a football. The graffiti sprayed on the wall behind them made Alfie catch his breath.

At the centre was a large red X.

Alfie turned to Francis who was tying up his shoe laces. "Have you ever heard of someone called Mr. X?"

"Mr. X? Everyone's heard of him around here," Francis said. "He's a proper hard man. No one messes with him."

Alfie chewed on his lip. He thought Mr. X had been something his aunt and uncle had made up, like the bogeyman.

"So he's real then?" Alfie asked.

"Oh, he's real all right." Francis grinned. "Do you want to see where he lives?"

Alfie blinked. See him? God, no, that was the last thing he wanted.

But Francis had sensed his fear. "Are you too scared? You're such a baby, Alfie."

"I'm not scared. You're the one who's scared to jump a few steps on a skateboard," Alfie said. "Anyway, I bet he's not even real."

"All right then. Come with me," Francis said, standing up. "I'll show you."

CHAPTER THREE

ALFIE RELUCTANTLY FOLLOWED FRANCIS TO the entrance to Victoria House. The door was slightly ajar. It was dim inside and Alfie felt the hairs on the back of his neck stand up. He didn't want to do this.

"I need to get home," Alfie said. "My aunt will be back from work soon."

"It will only take a minute," Francis said, striding ahead.

A noise ahead of them made Alfie jump. He flattened himself against the wall by the entrance.

A gang of younger kids ran past them. Halloween wasn't until next week, but they were wearing costumes already.

One of the smaller kids wore a white sheet with cutouts for his eyes. Only trouble was he hadn't quite gotten the hang of it. He had the eye holes on the top of his head. Alfie winced as the little kid tripped over the trailing sheet, but he was soon up again, chasing after his friends.

Alfie straightened up, his cheeks burning. He was glad Francis hadn't seen his reaction. What was the matter with him? Scared of a group of little kids. Pathetic.

Francis was climbing the steps to the doorway, babbling on about how he could show Alfie where Mr. X lived.

"I heard about him from Tim who lives on the second floor. Apparently, Mr. X did him a favour."

"What's Mr. X's real name?" Alfie asked.

Francis laughed. "Well, he doesn't want people to know his real name, does he? What would be the point in that? He'd have all sorts of people turning up to ask him for favours."

Alfie shook his head. He was sure Francis was making this up. Either that, or he'd been watching too much TV.

"Are you ready, Alfie? Are you sure you don't want to chicken out?" Francis laughed.

Alfie scowled. "Just get on with it."

Alfie didn't believe Francis knew Mr. X. He was just trying to scare him. He wanted him to run away so he could tease him about it the next day at school. Francis often made up stories, and he had a fascination with Halloween. Last year, Francis had dressed up as the killer from the film *Scream*. He loved horror films and was always trying to get Alfie to watch them too, laughing when Alfie jumped at the scary bits.

Francis grinned broadly as he stopped by the door to Victoria House. He grabbed the handle.

"Well, here we are." Francis cleared his throat. He suddenly looked a little less sure of himself.

He pushed open the door. "Are you sure you want to see where he lives?"

Alfie nodded. He just wanted to get this over with. If he didn't get home before five-thirty, his aunt would be furious.

Francis licked his lips. "All right. Follow me."

They took the lift up to the fourth floor, and when the lift doors opened, Francis gave Alfie yet another chance to back out. Alfie shook his head. Now he was convinced Francis had made up the whole thing. There was no Mr. X. Francis just wanted Alfie to be impressed.

Of course, Mr. X couldn't be true. He was just some mythical figure designed to scare children into behaving themselves. It was like his grandma telling Alfie that Santa wouldn't leave him any presents if he were naughty.

Alfie smiled as he followed Francis out of the lift and along the corridor. Alfie wrinkled his nose. It smelled of boiled cabbage up here.

Francis stopped when they reached flat number forty-two.

He raised his hand to knock, but the door was slightly ajar.

"It's open," Francis whispered. He pushed the door open a little further.

There was a strange music drifting out from the flat, a mixture of chanting voices and drums.

Francis slipped his head round the door.

"What is it?" Alfie tapped his shoulder.

But Francis didn't move.

Alfie moved forward to see what Francis was looking at.

At the same time, Francis took a step backwards, bumping into Alfie.

Alfie's nose cracked hard on the back of Francis's shoulder. "Ow, watch where you are going."

But Francis didn't answer. Instead he carried on backing up, pushing Alfie back out of the flat.

"What are you doing?" Alfie asked, rubbing his sore nose.

Francis ignored Alfie. His eyes were wide, and his jaw was slack as he stared at the entrance to the flat.

Alfie had had enough of this. Francis was just winding him up.

"I'm going," he said.

With luck, he'd get home before his aunt, and she'd never find out he hadn't gone straight home after school.

Francis's jaw worked up and down a couple of times. Now he was really going over the top. He looked like a goldfish, opening and shutting his mouth like that.

"What's the matter with you?" Alfie asked, as he pushed past Francis to look inside the flat.

It was hard to see anything at first. It was dark outside, and the only light in the flat came from one flickering candle.

As Alfie's eyes adjusted to the darkness, he saw the door opened directly into a sparsely furnished living room.

In the centre of the room, a large hooded figure crouched over something on the floor.

It took Alfie a moment to realise the thing on the floor was a person. A person who was lying face down on the bare floorboards.

Alfie blinked trying to take it all in.

The hooded figure picked up a huge knife and slashed the air. The blade seemed to glow in the candlelight. He murmured words Alfie didn't understand.

The hooded figure set down the knife and picked up a small wooden dish. He dipped a hand in the bowl's contents, and as he withdrew his hand, dark liquid dripped from his fingertips.

He used his fingers to smear the dark substance across the victim's forehead.

Alfie took a step back. They had to get out of here before they were seen.

The hooded figure grunted as he flipped the body over. The person on the floor didn't make any effort to escape. Was he dead? Unconscious?

The hooded figure grabbed the knife again. This time there were no words.

He pressed the blade to the victim's shoulder. As the blade scraped its way over flesh, the first crimson flush of blood appeared on the man's back.

Alfie held his breath. He tried to move back. But Francis was behind him, rigid with fear, and Alfie couldn't get past. If they could just get out now without being seen, it would be okay.

He shoved Francis who stumbled against the wall.

Alfie could see the exit. He tugged at Francis's hand and tried to pull him into the corridor.

Francis started to shake, then he made a low gurgling sound that made Alfie panic. Alfie clamped a hand over Francis's mouth.

But it was no good.

Francis's scream bubbled to the surface. It echoed around the walls of the corridor, distorting the scream into something terrifying.

The hooded figure slowly looked up from his task and directly at Alfie and Francis.

He couldn't see the figure's face beneath the hood, but Alfie was positive he could see theirs.

Alfie frantically yanked on Francis's arm. But Francis wouldn't move.

"Come on. We need to get out of here," Alfie hissed.

At the back of his mind, Alfie had a nagging hope that this was all some kind of joke. But when the hooded figure began to walk towards them, Alfie felt his stomach twist.

Alfie pulled again on Francis's arm, but he was completely unresponsive.

Alfie let go of Francis's arm and ran down the corridor. He was running so fast he crashed into the door leading to the stairwell. He was back on his feet in an instant, taking the stairs three at a time, jumping and stumbling as he headed for the exit.

Why hadn't Francis moved? Had it all been a stupid Halloween trick? Alfie wasn't going to hang around to find out. If Francis wanted to scare him, he had succeeded.

Alfie reached the bottom of the staircase, and a moment later, he burst out into the square. He didn't pause for breath. He took off at a sprint and didn't stop running until he'd reached his aunt and uncle's flat.

CHAPTER FOUR

WALTER HARWOOD JUMPED. THE SOLES of his Wellington boots slapped against the black mud of the riverbed as he landed.

He stood still for a moment, breathing in the sharp tang of the river, savouring it as he looked out at the inky, darkness of the River Thames.

He grinned. He had stayed away for too long.

The sun would be up soon, and he would have to share London with the rest of the population, but for now, he had it to himself, and he loved it.

He carefully pulled the tatty old metal detector from its case. He couldn't believe his father had kept it. How many years had it been since the old man had used it? Fifteen? Twenty?

Walter inspected the machine and tightened a screw on the handle. It was funny how something like this could hold so many memories.

Walter had sat stony-faced for weeks beside his father's bed at the hospital. He'd arranged the funeral and greeted his dad's old friends with a polite *thanks for coming, Dad would have appreciated it,* at the wake afterwards.

He'd managed to hold it together until five days after the funeral. That was when he had decided it was time to clear out his father's flat.

Even then, he'd been okay, methodically sorting through his dad's possessions and separating them into piles for the charity shop and piles for his sister.

His steely self-control had stayed with him until he'd reached the top shelf of his father's wardrobe. His fingers had closed around a long thin object. At first, he couldn't place it. Then a moment later, he realised what it was, and the memories came flooding back with force.

Walter gasped and flopped down to sit on the floor with his back propped against the bed. He unzipped the case to reveal the metal detector.

He remembered when his dad had first bought it. He'd phoned Walter, full of excitement, eager to tell him about his new toy. He'd wanted Walter to go with him to the river to test it out.

Walter leaned forward and rested his head on his knees. He had told his dad he was too busy. Fool. What he wouldn't give now for just one more day with his dad.

He blinked back tears as he rubbed his thumb over a rough patch of rust on the metal.

It had been something they'd done together. Mudlarking on the Thames. Walter could still remember the first time his father had taken him down to the river.

Walter's head had been full of the treasure they were going to discover.

So the years had passed with Walter and his father combing the river at low tide, searching for their treasure. Walter couldn't remember when he had stopped or why. His father had kept on visiting the Thames, but Walter had grown interested in other things.

Their first discovery had been a clay pipe, white as bone. Later, Walter came to realise that the pipes were a common find, but on that day, he was full of excitement as he thought he'd discovered an ancient pirate's pipe. Cupped in his father's strong hands, it had looked so fragile.

Walter shook his head at the memory. When had his father's hands changed from the strong ones that held the pipe, to the shaking, weak hands that had clutched Walter's in the hospital?

Alone in his father's bedroom, Walter had lowered his head and cried.

Now, Walter looked down at the pristine, silty sand beneath his feet. There could be anything down there. Maybe old coins or buckles. Things that had been lost for years. The river could wash up things it had claimed centuries ago.

Walter smiled. Maybe today would be the day he uncovered his big find, the sort of treasure he'd dreamed about as a boy.

On every trip, Walter's father used to say he had a feeling in his bones that their big discovery was just around the corner.

Walter took another breath of the tangy air and looked

up and down the beach. He was out of sight from the road above, which was a good thing. You were supposed to have a permit for mudlarking these days.

As he took a step forward, the mud sucked at the soles of his wellingtons. The silt here could be notoriously tricky, and it was easy to get stuck, especially when the tide went out as far as this. The trick was to keep moving and never stand still for too long.

His Wellington boots made squelching noises with each step, as he set off towards the river line. He would need to keep an eye on the tide.

The tide was low, which meant he could explore more of the riverbed. Walter held the metal detector in front of him. He'd begun to move it slowly back and forth when something caught the corner of his eye—something that shouldn't be there.

He turned, frowning at the object. Back when Walter used to walk up and down this stretch of river with his father, he'd seen all sorts of discarded rubbish. Pushchairs and shoes were popular. Sadly the river was a bit of a dumping ground. It always had been. Even back when the Victorian street urchins had been the mudlarks, earning their living by digging in the riverbed, searching for discarded coal and other things they could sell.

Walter walked towards the large, black object. As he got closer, the silt and sand sucked hard on his Wellington boots, making each step slow and ponderous.

As he got closer he saw that it was a black refuse sack. The water lapped at the bottom of the bag. Someone had obviously dumped their rubbish in the river. Some people had no respect.

Walter kneeled down beside the bag and yanked at the black plastic. It was very heavy, which took Walter by surprise. He couldn't even lift it. *What the hell was in there?*

It was hard to see. The sun was only just cresting over London, highlighting the buildings in the distance and glinting off the Shard.

Walter peered down at the refuse sack. It was sealed with brown parcel tape. Walter fumbled with it for a moment, but the tape was too strong, and he couldn't rip it.

Sod that for a game of soldiers, Walter thought, and decided to create a hole in the plastic. He pulled out his Leatherman penknife and carefully cut a hole in the plastic.

A foul odour seeped out immediately. As Walter ripped open the hole wider, he choked.

He'd seen plenty of things dumped in the river, but this was a first. Walter careered backwards, landing on his back-side in the soft silt. The smell overwhelmed him, and he felt the need to vomit.

He put his hands down to push himself up, but the silt gripped and sucked at his hands.

The river wasn't willing to give up its victim. Walter started to panic. He imagined himself sinking into the silt along with the dead body.

Stop being such a bloody fool, Walter told himself. He needed to stop panicking. He wasn't going to get anywhere at this rate. He needed to stay calm and spread his weight over the sand.

Carefully extracting each of his hands, Walter shifted his

weight. He rolled over onto his front and spreadeagled himself, trying to spread his weight over as much area as possible.

He whimpered with relief as the tight suction eased its grip on his limbs, and he was able to get up to his knees and then back on his feet.

He was covered with the grimy brown mud from the riverbed. Walter looked back at the black plastic bag and blinked a couple of times.

A human hand was sticking out from the hole he had created. Walter swallowed. The hand almost looked as if it were waving at him.

Walter's father had always said the next big find was just around the corner. But Walter was pretty sure he hadn't meant this.

CHAPTER FIVE

DETECTIVE SERGEANT MACKINNON DESCENDED THE slippery steps. These days the steps down to the river didn't get much use, but each step had a dip in the middle, created by the traffic of previous generations of Londoners. He gripped the thin handrail, but even that disappeared halfway down.

Once he was safely down the treacherous steps, Mackinnon saw that the tide had turned, and water was already lapping the bank where the body had been discovered. The team had needed to work quickly to log as much evidence as possible before the river claimed it.

Thankfully, most of the initial work had been completed, and the pathologist was getting ready to have the body moved. The crime scene staff were packing up their equipment and loading it back into the van at the top of the river.

DI Tyler was on the phone gesturing with his right hand

as was his habit. Mackinnon thought he heard Brookbank's name mentioned and decided not to approach Tyler yet.

DC Charlotte Brown was talking to one of the crime scene photographers. When she saw Mackinnon she waved, and he walked over to her.

"Nasty one," she said, holding out her mobile phone.

Mackinnon angled the phone so he could see the image on the screen clearly. It looked like a flat disc of wood. "That was found in the boy's mouth?"

Charlotte nodded. "It was in a red velvet pouch. Tucked in his right cheek." She raised a hand to her own cheek.

"Any idea what it's for?" Mackinnon asked.

"Not yet." Charlotte zoomed in on the image. "See that. It's marked with a cross."

Mackinnon studied it for a few moments, then said, "What about the victim?"

"Young black male. No ID as yet."

"How young?"

Charlotte shrugged. "Hard to say. Pathologist guessed at mid to late teens."

"How was he killed?"

"Not clear on that yet. There are stab wounds, a couple of them might have been fatal, and his back has been slashed from shoulder to hip bone, diagonally on both sides. The knife wounds formed a cross just like on the wooden disc."

Mackinnon took in a breath of misty air and looked out over the water. Above them on the street, life was going on as usual. A red double-decker bus rolled by, and people rushed along the embankment in the fine drizzle, eager to get on their way. No one noticed the crime scene below.

DI Tyler put his phone in his pocket and gestured for everyone to gather round. Mackinnon and Charlotte headed towards him.

"Okay," Tyler said. "We will have a briefing back at the station, but I want you…" He pointed at Mackinnon. "… to go and see an expert on West African anthropology at Kings College London. I've just spoken with her on the phone. She's on the list, and the Metropolitan Police have used her before. I want you to take a photograph of that flat wooden thing we found in the boy's mouth and show it to the professor. Let's see whether she can shed any light on it."

DI Tyler turned to Charlotte. "I need you to look at missing persons. There's no ID on him, so whoever dumped him didn't want to make it easy for us, but he is a teenager. He is likely to have family. His parents are prob-ably looking for him. He's been in the drink for a couple of days, so someone must have noticed he's gone."

After Tyler finished assigning tasks, he gave Mackinnon the details for the anthropologist, and Charlotte sent a copy of the image of the wooden disc to Mackinnon's phone.

Mackinnon climbed the stone steps to the embankment and headed for the nearest underground station.

It took only ten minutes to get to the Strand, which was where the professor of African anthropology was based. Mackinnon scrolled through his phone to check the details Tyler had given him.

The anthropologist's name was Professor Matić. Mack-innon pondered over the name. It wasn't a name he'd come across before, but he didn't think it sounded West African in origin.

Mackinnon showed his ID at the reception desk in the front of the large Kings College building.

Students, scurrying between lectures, filled the grand entrance hall, and two open stairways curled upwards to the mezzanine level.

The chap on reception gave him directions to Professor Matić's office on the second floor.

As the students poured down the stairs, Mackinnon suddenly felt very old. They all looked too young to be at university.

He strolled along the corridor following the receptionist's instructions, but he couldn't find Professor Matić's office. When he reached the end of the corridor, there was a large lecture theatre. He peered inside, but there was no one in there.

He must have taken a wrong turn. He headed back the way he had come, and instead of turning right at the top of the staircase, he turned left, and two doors down, he found Professor Matić's office.

Mackinnon rapped on the door. There was no answer, and as he held up his hand to knock again someone walked behind him.

A young girl, hugging a ring binder to her chest and a rucksack slung over her shoulder, asked, "Are you looking for Professor Matić?"

Mackinnon nodded.

"She's taking a lecture now, but she should be nearly finished. I can take you to the lecture theatre if you want?"

Mackinnon thanked her and followed her to Professor Matić's class.

The girl pointed to a set of double doors, and Mackinnon stepped inside.

It was a large room, with staggered seating. The lights were dimmed, and a video was projecting onto a white screen at the front of the room.

At first, Mackinnon thought the people on the screen were dancing. Then he saw the glowing coals beneath their feet. Mackinnon winced.

A rhythmic beating of drums and a low chanting accompanied the recording.

"As you can see," a voice said, drawing Mackinnon's attention to the speaker, a tall woman standing by the projector. "The tribe appears to enter a trance-like state at this point, and according to the researchers who witnessed this event, they feel no pain."

Mackinnon guessed this was Professor Linda Matić. She was an attractive woman, in her late thirties or early forties with carefully styled shoulder-length blonde hair.

She flicked a switch on the projector, and the video disappeared from the screen. The sudden ending of the music left Mackinnon with the odd sensation that he could still hear the echo of the drums beating.

Behind Professor Matić, the screen was filled with images of various African sculptures and artefacts.

He glanced at his watch. Hopefully, this wouldn't take long. Professor Matić had a charismatic voice, and despite the size of the room, her voice carried right to the back. To Mackinnon's surprise all the students looked very interested. Quite a contrast to his university days when most of the students used lectures as an excuse to take forty winks.

But Mackinnon had to agree the subject was interesting. No doubt the mystery and legends of West Africa were more appealing than his degree course had been. Professor Matić talked her way through a couple more slides, and then she wrapped up the session and switched the lights back on.

As the students trudged up the steps past Mackinnon to get to the exits, he weaved his way through them to meet Professor Matić at the bottom.

She was packing her things together. As she reached to switch off her laptop, she raised an eyebrow. "Can I help you?"

Mackinnon showed her his ID. "Professor Matić, I am DS Mackinnon. I know you have helped the Metropolitan Police in the past, and we have a new case that could benefit from your expertise."

Professor Matić nodded. "I'll do my best to help," she said. "But I can't do much without caffeine. We can talk in my office if you don't mind getting coffee on the way."

Mackinnon nodded. "Sounds good to me."

They stopped at the university cafeteria, which was full of young students sipping coffees and eating large slices of cake.

Mackinnon's stomach growled, but he resisted the cake, opting for a black coffee.

On the way to Professor Matić's office, she told Mackinnon of her work with the Met. She had helped them on numerous occasions.

Her last case had been helping the police following the murder of an albino child.

"The police suspected she had been sacrificed, and parts of her body used for a variety of rituals that were supposed to bring good luck," Professor Matić said.

The professor noted the horrified look on Mackinnon's face.

"It's a very rare occurrence," she said. "A very small minority believe that albino body parts are more potent, and so the rituals they use them for have more power. There have been multiple reports of abductions of albino children from small villages in Tanzania."

Professor Matić handed Mackinnon her coffee so she could unlock the door to her office.

Professor Matić's office was filled to the brim. There was barely enough space for her desk and two chairs.

She apologised and lifted a large wooden sculpture off one of the chairs. The sculpture was fashioned from dark wood and had been shaped into a grotesque figure with a gaping mouth.

"Sorry," she said. "I'm attempting some cataloguing this week, but I fear I am fighting a losing battle."

She nodded for Mackinnon to sit down in the seat vacated by the statue.

Mackinnon took a moment to take it all in. Every available surface from her desk to the windowsill was covered in artefacts. Even the floor had a variety of statues interspersed between the piles of paper.

Once the professor had taken a seat, too, Mackinnon pulled out his phone.

"If you can, Professor, I've got a picture of something I'd like you to identify," he said.

"Please, call me Linda," she said, leaning forward to view the image.

Mackinnon zoomed in on a picture of the round, flat wooden object that had been found in the victim's mouth and handed his phone to Linda.

She pulled her glasses down and squinted at the image, holding it one way and then the other. She pursed her lips as she studied it.

Mackinnon waited for a moment, then said, "Do you recognise it? Is it anything to do with a West African religion?"

Professor Matić handed him back the phone. "I've never seen anything like it before. It's quite a crudely made object. Handmade I would guess. Why did you think to bring it to me?"

"The disc was found in the mouth of a murder victim, a young boy. It was in a red velvet pouch," Mackinnon said. "We've estimated the victim to be mid-teens. But we've not identified him yet."

Professor Matić ran her hands over her face and sighed. "Oh, that's awful. Would I be right in thinking you are considering Voodoo?"

Mackinnon didn't respond.

"I can't say I have ever seen anything like it. Sometimes items are left as an offering to the spirits, but I've never seen anything like this disc before. I mean, maybe if it had been bones or something similar… I'm not sure, but I think somebody could be trying to throw you off track."

"You think someone is trying to make it *look* like Voodoo?"

Professor Linda Matić shrugged. "Possibly," she said. "I have made a career of studying religions, including Voodoo, but even I don't know everything."

She frowned. "I can give you the contact details of a man I've been working with. He's helping me with my new book. He's a religious leader who practices Voodoo. He lives in Poplar, and he's well known in the community, so if anyone would be able to identify this object, I think it would be him."

Mackinnon nodded. "That would be very helpful, thank you."

"He is known as the Oracle," Linda said and scribbled down his details on a slip of paper.

Mackinnon took the piece of paper, thanked Professor Linda Matić again and headed back out onto the Strand.

He looked at his watch. Meeting with Professor Linda Matić had taken an hour, and he would have missed the briefing, but an hour was a long time in a case like this. The team might have had a breakthrough and made huge progress by now. He hoped so.

If not, they'd have to pin their hopes on getting some answers from Linda Matić's Oracle.

CHAPTER SIX

MACKINNON CALLED TYLER STRAIGHT AWAY, giving him the bad news that the professor hadn't been able to identify the object found in the victim's mouth.

He'd sweetened the news by telling Tyler that he had the contact details for a local Vodun Oracle, named Germaine Okoro.

"That's something at least," Tyler had said. "We haven't managed to identify the boy yet. I've got most of the team working on that, but I'll get Charlotte to meet you at Okoro's address."

Mackinnon met up with Charlotte at Mile End Station, and they walked to the address in Poplar, East London.

Number thirty-six Queen Elizabeth Walk was an attractive, three-storey terraced house. It stood out from others in the street in a good way. There were pretty window boxes with flowers still in bloom underneath the ground floor windows. The door was painted a dark glossy red, and the brass doorknob and letterbox gleamed.

They were surprised when a young man opened the door. He was surely too young to be the Oracle.

Mackinnon had pictured an older man, dressed in robes and a headdress, but the man who stood before them wore a green hoodie, low slung jeans and bright red socks. His hair was closely cropped to his scalp, and lines had been shaved into the side of his hairline, above his ears.

"We were hoping to speak with Germaine Okoro," Charlotte said, holding up her ID. "DC Brown and DS Mackinnon of the City of London police."

The man's eyes widened, and he tilted his chin. "My father's in the garden," he said. "Come in. Do you want to wait inside and I'll go and get him, or you can go out to the garden and speak with him there."

"The garden is fine," Mackinnon said.

"I'm Kwame," he said, opening the front door wide so Charlotte and Mackinnon could enter. "I take it you haven't come with bad news?"

"No, it's nothing like that. Your father is expecting us. I called ahead. He's helping us with an investigation."

Kwame nodded, and they followed him through to the living room.

The house was bigger than it looked from the outside. The living room was open plan, with a couple of leather sofas behind a chrome and glass dining table. Four black, leather chairs lined up on each side of the table.

The floors were polished wood, and the walls were painted white. On some of the walls, there were abstract black and white photographs, framed with black wood. The overall look of the room was very modern and not what Mackinnon had been expecting.

He wasn't sure exactly what he had been expecting. Perhaps something a little more traditional. Maybe some African artefacts laying around.

Kwame headed to a double set of French doors that led out onto the garden, and called for his dad. As Mackinnon stepped outside he saw Germaine Okoro straighten up from a flower bed and raise a hand in welcome.

He had been dead-heading fuchsias. Mackinnon frowned. Fuchsias still flowering in October? Mackinnon wasn't much of a gardener, but wasn't that unusual?

Kwame called out from behind them. "Can I get you something to drink? Coffee or tea?"

Mackinnon and Charlotte both asked for a coffee, and Kwame nodded and shut the doors behind him.

Mackinnon took another look around the garden, which was more country cottage than inner city. It was amazing, so green and so many flowers were still blooming. Definitely odd for this time of year.

They walked across the short area of lawn until they reached Germaine Okoro. Mackinnon held out his hand. "Thanks for seeing us," he said and introduced himself and Charlotte.

As they shook hands, Charlotte said, "Professor Linda Matić suggested you might be able to help us."

Mr. Okoro nodded. "Yes. You mentioned something on the phone about a wooden object?"

Charlotte nodded, pulled out her mobile and scrolled

through the phone until she got an image of the flat, wooden, circular object that had been found in the victim's mouth.

"This is it." She held out the phone and explained how one side of the wooden disc was plain, and the other side was marked with a cross. "Do you have any idea what it's for?"

The Oracle was silent for some moments as he studied it.

Mackinnon felt his stomach sink when the Oracle finally let out a deep breath and shook his head. "I'm sorry, I've never seen anything like that before. Are you assuming it is something to do with the Vodun religion?"

Mackinnon shook his head. "We are not assuming anything. It was found in the victim's mouth. We believe it must have some significance."

The Oracle nodded his head. "Of course. However, I don't think it's Voodoo. Perhaps it is a ritual of some significance, but it's no kind of Voodoo I've ever heard of."

The Oracle looked down at the vivid pink fuchsias he had been tending when they arrived.

"Tell me, detective, how much do you know about the religion?"

"Not very much, really," Mackinnon admitted.

"Probably only what you know from Hollywood or dramatic news stories in the press," the Oracle said. "But it's only as strange as some other forms of religion seem to outsiders. Drinking the blood of Christ, for example. Some might consider that a little macabre."

Mackinnon didn't want to get into a religious debate.

After talking to Professor Matić, Mackinnon had a feeling that the Voodoo angle in this case could be a red herring.

The Oracle turned to Charlotte. "Our religion creates a very strong social network. Women play an essential role. They perform baptisms, weddings and funerals. It's really not the scary black magic that most people associate with Voodoo."

"The murder victim," the Oracle asked, turning to Mackinnon, "do you mind if I ask who it was?"

Mackinnon took a deep breath and breathed in the green scent of the garden. Although the sun was bright today, it had turned colder this afternoon, and he wished he'd worn a warmer coat.

"We haven't identified the victim yet," Mackinnon said. "We know he's male. We think he's early teens."

The Oracle's face crinkled. "How terrible. I do know a teacher who belongs to our group. He works locally. Of course, that's assuming the boy is local…He may not be…" The Oracle trailed off.

"Thank you. It would be useful to get the teacher's contact details," Charlotte said.

"Is there any evidence to say where the boy is from?" the Oracle asked.

Mackinnon shook his head. "Not yet."

Mackinnon remembered a case that hit the headlines a few years back. The torso of a young boy had been found in the River Thames. The boy had been named by police as Adam. Scientific studies had shown that he had actually been born in Nigeria, and the police working the case had concluded he'd been smuggled into Britain.

It was amazing what science could do now. It was possible to trace someone's origins and find out things about them by the food they had eaten.

Mackinnon hoped they wouldn't need to do a detailed study like that with this case because that would mean a long investigation, and as everyone knew, the longer an investigation took, the colder the case got.

Kwame padded up behind them, holding two cups in his right hand and one in his left. He handed a coffee to Mackinnon, then one to Charlotte, and then one to his father.

"So, what have you done this time, Dad?" He winked and smiled, but the Oracle frowned.

"Your father was just helping us with some enquiries," Charlotte said.

Kwame nodded and grinned. He put his hands in his pockets and gazed down at his trainers.

"He's been very helpful and has given us an insight into the Voodoo religion," Charlotte explained.

"The mumbo jumbo, you mean," Kwame said and chuckled to himself.

Mackinnon frowned. Well, that was awkward. He saw a flash of anger flicker across the father's face.

Mackinnon cleared his throat. "Perhaps we could get the name and address of the contact you suggested, Mr. Okoro. The teacher?"

"Of course," the Oracle said, mustering his dignity. "I'll just be one moment."

Kwame watched his father walk back towards the house

and shook his head. "I shouldn't wind him up, I know. But he takes it all so seriously."

"And you don't?" Charlotte asked.

"Please. Are you serious? I was born in London. I went to school in London, and now, I'm at university studying biology. Real science. Why would I have time for any of that?"

Charlotte didn't reply, and the Oracle returned with a handwritten note.

"Here you are. He's a teacher at Poplar Comprehensive. His name is William Xander.

"He helps underprivileged children, too, not just the ones that go to his school. I think he runs some kind of after school club as well. It's a long shot, but he might know something. He is a good man and a member of our congregation."

Mackinnon took the note. "Thank you. I have to say you have a beautiful garden. How do you get the fuchsias to bloom so late in the season?"

The Oracle gave Mackinnon a sly smile. "That's all down to the fertiliser. I use the best fertiliser in the world."

"Oh, really? What fertiliser is that?" Mackinnon asked, thinking he might get some. Chloe's garden was huge, and some of the plants were looking a little weathered. They could definitely do with a helping hand.

"Why, blood of course," the Oracle said. "The essence of life."

Mackinnon suppressed a shudder, and shot a horrified glance at Charlotte as the Oracle turned to lead them out of the garden and back through the house.

Charlotte shrugged. "My parents were always very into gardening before they moved to Spain. They used a mix of blood and bone meal. They sell it prepackaged these days."

They were nearly at the front door when the Oracle turned to Charlotte.

He paused and shivered.

"I have…" He put a hand on her arm. "I have a very bad feeling about this."

He raised his head to the ceiling, and his eyes rolled back to show the whites. His eyelids fluttered.

They stood there in silence for a moment, and then his eyes snapped open, and he gazed at Charlotte.

And in a low voice, he said, "Be careful."

CHAPTER SEVEN

"WELL, THAT WAS CREEPY," CHARLOTTE said as the door closed behind them. She rubbed her arm.

"I don't think he meant to be creepy," Mackinnon said. "But a young boy is dead, and some sicko put a weird wooden object in his mouth. I think most people would have a bad feeling about that."

Charlotte shivered and wrapped her coat tightly around her. "So, what do you want to do now? Shall we go to the school and see this teacher, Mr. Xander?"

Mackinnon shook his head. "Let's go back to the station first and check in with Tyler. There might have been some developments, and we'll see what Tyler wants us to do next."

It took twenty minutes for them to get back to Wood Street Station. They entered through the reception, passing a couple of people sitting on the plastic chairs.

Mackinnon nodded to the duty sergeant and swiped his

access card to get into the main police-only area of the station.

They found Collins nursing a cup of coffee at his desk, staring at the computer.

"Any news?" Mackinnon asked.

Collins nodded and put down his coffee. "We've got an ID, I think. The parents are here now. They reported their son missing on Friday night." He took a deep breath. "They are formally identifying him now."

Mackinnon winced, after all that time in the Thames, it wouldn't be an easy identification. Not that those sorts of things were ever easy.

Collins took another sip of coffee, which made Mackinnon crave a cup of his own. "His parents say they think he fell in with a bad crowd. He's been acting out for the last six months or so."

It was great that they had an identification, but he couldn't imagine the hell the boy's parents were going through right now.

In his pocket, he touched the slip of paper the Oracle had given him. Now they had an ID for the victim, they would probably have more reliable leads to go on.

"So, how did you get on?" Collins asked them.

"We didn't have much luck," Mackinnon said. "I spoke with Professor Matić. She was helpful and obviously an expert on the Voodoo religion, but she didn't recognise the bit of wood found in the boy's mouth.

"She gave us details for a contact of hers, a kind of religious leader in the local community who practices Voodoo. His real name is Germaine Okoro, but they call him the

Oracle. Unfortunately, he didn't recognise the object either. Both he and the professor say they don't think it's of any religious significance."

Collins looked disappointed. "So, no leads at all?"

"Well, Germaine Okoro gave us the name of a teacher who helps underprivileged children in the area," Charlotte said. "He's also a member of the Oracle's group, so we were going to go and pay him a visit, but I guess we've got stronger leads now the boy has been identified."

Collins turned to the computer and scrolled through the pages of notes on the database. "The boy's name is Francis Eze. Twelve years old, and he went to Poplar Comprehensive."

Mackinnon nodded. Poplar Comprehensive was the school William Xander taught at, so it would still be worth paying him a visit. The lead may not be such a bust after all.

"I'm going to go and get myself a coffee," Mackinnon said. "And then we'll check in with Tyler."

Mackinnon left the office area and headed up to the cafeteria, deep in thought. He climbed the stairs two at a time, and when he reached the second level, he paused. In front of him, a middle-aged black couple was headed in the opposite direction.

There was no doubt in Mackinnon's mind that they were the boy's parents. They seemed to be surrounded by other officers, leading the way, but there was a hush around them, as if everyone was feeling the weight of their grief.

The mother walked rigidly. Her eyes were wide and unblinking.

Her husband was the complete opposite. He seemed to

have a need to keep moving. He shoved his hands in his pockets, only to move them again, running them through his hair. Then his right hand moved down to cover his mouth. His head whipped one way and then the other, as if he were trying to take it all in.

Behind them, their family liaison officer followed. It was Rosialie Estes.

Rosialie was a fantastic FLO. Few officers were suited to the role, but she had a calm, unobtrusive way of dealing with people that made them feel reassured. It was an incredibly difficult task. Not many individuals could enter a family home after a tragedy and ask the most personal questions without appearing intrusive.

Mackinnon had worked with Rosialie before. He nodded as he caught her eye. It wasn't much consolation for the parents, but at least, they had some support.

He didn't want the parents to feel they were the object of everyone's interest, so he kept his head down and carried on towards the cafeteria.

He couldn't imagine how they were feeling. What kind of a monster would do something like that to a twelve-year-old boy?

CHAPTER EIGHT

ALFIE WAS SCARED.

HE HADN'T seen Francis since Friday. He'd tried loads of times to call him on his mobile, but Francis hadn't answered, and he didn't dare leave a message.

He didn't know what to do. Was this part of some elaborate wind up by Francis?

He'd tried to convince himself of that at the weekend, but now it was Monday, and Francis hadn't come to school. There was no way his parents would let him skive off.

Alfie hunched one shoulder, yanked up his rucksack and walked towards the Maths block. There were only two more lessons until school was finished, then Alfie decided he would go round to Francis's flat and speak to his mum.

Francis's mum had always been nice to Alfie. She gave him cookies and milk whenever he went to call on Francis.

Maybe Francis was sick? Yes, Alfie tried to convince

himself, that's probably what it was. Francis would be back at school tomorrow.

A quiet voice in the back of Alfie's mind said: *What if the hooded figure had caught Francis?*

Alfie hadn't looked back to see if Francis was okay. He'd tried to pull Francis with him, but the idiot wouldn't move.

It wasn't his fault.

What would the hooded figure have done to Francis if he'd caught him?

No, he couldn't have caught him. Francis was a fast runner. He'd won the two-hundred metres on sports day last summer.

What if the man caught Francis? Did that mean Alfie would be next?

Alfie rubbed his eyes. No. Francis must be okay. He would have run away, too. Alfie would go and see him after school. Francis would probably be in bed with a bug or something.

As Alfie rounded the corner and started to walk underneath the covered walkway, outside the Maths block, he saw a group of older students gathered around the entrance, talking excitedly in hushed whispers.

"I heard he'd been stabbed fifty times."

"No, that's not right. I heard he'd just been stabbed once in the eye."

"You're all wrong," said an older girl Alfie recognised as Farzana Patani. "He had his throat cut." She said the words in a matter of fact way.

Alfie didn't know who they were talking about, but he felt a light, cold sweat breaking out along his forehead.

As he got closer, he could hear more of their conversation, and he knew for certain they were talking about Francis.

"Apparently, he didn't come home on Friday," a tall girl said. "Then they found his body all cut up into little pieces."

"What? No, that's not right. You're making that up," one of the older boys said.

"I am not," the girl said. "What would you know anyway?"

Just as Alfie passed them he heard one of the children say. "The police are here. They're gonna want to question all of us."

Alfie froze and turned to look at the speaker. It was Farzana Patani.

"Alfie!" Farzana called out to him. She walked towards him. Her eyes were soft, and she put a hand on his arm.

Alfie had heard of Farzana. She was captain of the school netball team, but she had never spoken to Alfie before.

"I'm sorry about Francis," she said. "Have you spoken to the police?"

Alfie shook his head vigorously.

"Well, they're here. I just saw them going into the headmaster's office, and they will want to speak to you. You were his best friend, weren't you?"

For a moment Alfie couldn't think straight. This had to be a mistake. He didn't want to speak to the police. *What if Mr. X found out and came after him?*

Alfie shrugged and tried to look as if he wasn't bothered

about the police. He walked on, passing the doors to the Maths block. He didn't want to go to class now. If he went to Maths, they would know where to find him.

"Hey, Alfie, where are you going? You need to go to the headmaster's office." Farzana Patani called after him.

Alfie ignored her, walking faster and faster. He cut back around the side of the Maths block and jogged over the playing field until he reached the big square building that housed the school's gym.

He could hear the squeak of trainers and the slam of balls against the hard surface as he entered.

The year eights were having a double session of PE. Alfie sneaked by, ducking his head under the small window in the door so he wouldn't be seen.

He headed for the stairs. He needed to get somewhere quiet where he could think and decide what to do next. The boys' changing rooms would be empty.

He opened the door to the changing room slowly and paused, listening, but there was no one inside.

Clothes hung on pegs, and the floor was scattered with school shoes that had been hastily removed. Alfie sighed with relief and carried his schoolbag over to the furthest bench, dumping it on the floor. He sat on the smooth wooden bench, leaning back against one of the lockers.

The gym changing rooms smelt of sweaty socks overlaid with the heavy smell of powdery deodorant, but Alfie didn't mind. At least he was alone. He was safe for now, and no one would think to look for him here.

He could still hear the muffled sounds of the year eights playing basketball downstairs. What was he going to do?

He couldn't be seen talking to the police as Mr. X might find out and come after him.

He wouldn't be safe at home either. His aunt was always saying that Mr. X was the only one who could sort Alfie out and drive away his evil spirits. If he told them about this, his aunt would probably hand him straight over to Mr. X.

Alfie pulled his feet up to the bench and hugged his knees against his chest.

He needed to make a plan. He couldn't avoid the police forever, especially not when they came to his school.

Maybe he could leave London. He could go to his grandma's in Southend. Surely she wouldn't turn Alfie away if he explained.

Just when Alfie thought he might have stumbled on the answer to his problems, he realised he had no money.

He searched the pockets of his school trousers and stared at the small collection of coins. He had enough for a portion of chips but definitely not enough to pay his fare to Southend.

Maybe he could just avoid the police today. He knew his aunt kept some money in a jar in the kitchen. Alfie could take that and leave tomorrow morning.

His grandma always promised he would be able to visit, but she'd only rung Alfie once after leaving him with his aunt and uncle, and he hadn't wanted to ask about visiting with his aunt standing over his shoulder.

He wondered what his grandma was doing now, and how his little brother Mickey was getting on at his new school. He wished she'd taken him to Southend. He would have liked to have lived by the sea.

Alfie looked around the changing room at the jackets and bags that were unattended. There was another way… He could take the money.

Surely with all the bags in here, he'd be able to scrape up enough money for his fare.

Alfie got to his feet and moved towards the first jacket and then stopped. This would be stealing… and that would be very wrong.

He put a thumbnail in his mouth and chewed. If he paid the money back later, it wasn't really stealing.

And besides, they were probably only going to use this money to buy a chocolate bar or a can of Coke after school. It would mean a packet of sweets to them, but to Alfie, this could mean life or death. Surely that meant it was okay.

He moved towards a jacket, flung the arm out of the way and fumbled in one of the pockets.

Then he froze.

He heard footsteps in the corridor outside the changing room.

Alfie yanked back his hand as if he'd been burned. Who was that? There wasn't supposed to be anyone up here now. They were all supposed to be playing in the gym.

But the footsteps were getting closer. Alfie needed to hide, but where?

He looked around. There were coats and bags everywhere, but nothing really big enough to hide behind.

Then Alfie remembered the showers at the end of the changing rooms. He ran to the end of the large communal showers and ducked inside just as he heard the door squeak open.

Alfie held his breath. Maybe it was someone coming back because they had forgotten something. He mumbled a prayer, promising never to think about stealing again if he could just get out of here unseen.

He heard rustling. Yes, Alfie told himself. They're looking for something. When they find it they will leave.

But they didn't leave.

The footsteps stopped, and Alfie could hear a rasping breathing.

Alfie covered his face with his hands and crouched down. Please let whoever it is go without seeing me. *Please. Please. Please.*

For the longest time, there was no movement and no sound. Alfie began to think he was imagining things. Maybe whoever it was had left.

Alfie edged forward, putting a hand onto the slippery, white tiles. He poked his head around the corner to peer into the changing rooms.

Too late he realised the changing rooms were not empty.

Standing by the door, with his arms folded and legs apart, looking murderous, was Mr. Xander.

Alfie gasped and reeled backwards into the showers again, but it was too late.

Mr. Xander had seen him and was striding forward. Alfie could hear the sound of his shoes slapping the floor.

"What are you doing?" Mr. Xander asked. "Out." He jerked a thumb and looked angrily at the floor of the showers where Alfie's school shoes had made a muddy mess all over the tiles.

Alfie stood there staring up at him, eyes wide. He couldn't find any words.

"Well, what do you have to say for yourself? What are you doing in here?"

Alfie just shook his head. "N... n... nothing, sir. I thought I had PE."

Mr. Xander's eyes narrowed.

"I hope you haven't taken anything from in here that isn't yours, Alfie," Mr. Xander said.

Alfie shook his head. "I haven't."

"Empty out your pockets."

Alfie did as he was told, emptying out a piece of tissue, a pound coin and a twenty pence piece.

"Hmm," Mr. Xander said. "Coat pockets."

They were empty.

"And where's your bag?"

Alfie dutifully trotted over to get his bag and presented it to Mr. Xander who rifled through it, turfing out various textbooks and pens until he was satisfied Alfie had not stolen anything.

Alfie thought he looked almost disappointed.

"I'd better not catch you sneaking around here again, Alfie. What lesson are you really supposed to be in?"

Alfie looked down at his shoes. "Maths," he said.

Mr. Xander loomed over him and then bent over to put his face close to Alfie's. He had dark, intense eyes, and it felt as if he could see right inside Alfie's head.

Alfie winced and moved backwards. "I'm sorry, I won't do it again."

He picked up his bag and moved for the door.

"Wait. Where do you think you're going?"

Alfie chewed on his lip. "Back to my Maths class."

Mr. Xander shook his head. "No, you're not," he said. "You're coming with me."

CHAPTER NINE

POPLAR COMPREHENSIVE WAS A TATTY sixties building. The squat, square of the main block had been added to over the years. Temporary structures were tacked onto the sides of the concrete building. Mackinnon imagined they were only supposed to last five or ten years. They looked like they had been there a lot longer than that.

As Mackinnon walked with Tyler to the main entrance, they got plenty of gaping looks from the students. He wondered if they'd been pegged for police already. Probably.

Mackinnon and Tyler were welcomed by a harassed school secretary who let the headmaster know they were there.

"He won't be long," she said. "He's been taking phone calls from parents all morning. It's been manic here."

She stepped out from behind her desk, trying to smooth her hair with one hand. "Can I get you something to drink?" she asked, not really meaning it. The telephone on her desk gave a shrill ring. "Another one," she said, and her shoulders slumped.

They waited for a couple of minutes, listening to the school secretary try to reassure parents on the phone.

After she had put the phone down for the fourth time, she said, "He'll see you now. Sorry, you had to wait, but I'm sure you understand how busy we are today."

"Funny enough, we are pretty busy too," Tyler mumbled as they entered the headmaster's office.

The headmaster was a small man called Scott Hincklin. His suit seemed several sizes too big for him, and his over-sized, black faux leather chair had the unfortunate effect of making him appear even smaller.

"Please take a seat," he said, and Mackinnon and Tyler sat down.

Scott Hincklin scratched his jaw. He had a pointed face, and his skin was so pale Mackinnon could see a thin blue vein pulsing at his temple.

"Of course we've had dealings with the police before," Scott Hincklin said. "During my first year at the school, we had a stabbing outside the school gates. The victim wasn't actually a student, but anyone reading the newspaper articles wouldn't have known that. They didn't tell the whole story."

He shuffled a few papers on his desk. "I'm not really sure how I can help, but of course, if there's anything I can do…" He shrugged.

Tyler leaned forward. "What can you tell us about Francis Eze?" he asked.

"Well..." The headmaster scratched his chin, leaving red marks on his pale skin. "Not much I'm afraid. He'd been here for eighteen months, and he was in year eight. Francis wasn't an outstanding pupil, but then, he wasn't really a troublemaker either. I'm afraid sometimes middle-of-the-road children go unnoticed." He gave them a weak smile.

Mackinnon wasn't surprised. In a school this size, with at least three thousand students, it was unlikely that any of them would receive individual attention.

Tyler tried again. "I understand that the headmaster may not come into contact with every pupil individually, but there must be another teacher who spent more time with Francis. They might be able to help us with our enquiries."

The headmaster nodded. "Yes, of course. The best person to try would be Mr. Xander. He was Francis's head of year."

"That would be helpful," Mackinnon said. "What about Francis's form tutor?"

"Unfortunately, Francis's form tutor is on maternity leave, and we've had a succession of temporary staff in that role. None of them were here very long..."

"Great," Tyler said, not hiding his annoyance. "If it's not too much trouble, we'd also like to speak with the students in Francis's year."

The headmaster blanched. "I'm not sure about that... I'd have to get permission from the parents. I can't just let you interrogate them."

"We are not planning on interrogating anyone, Mr.

Hincklin. We just want to find out what happened to Francis," Mackinnon said.

Scott Hincklin ran a hand through his fair hair, and then rubbed his eyes.

"Of course... I didn't mean... That is to say... It's just such a horrible thing isn't it, twelve-years-old." He stared down at his desk. "I'll have to arrange counselling sessions for the students. Such a horrible thing to happen..."

Scott Hincklin took a deep breath and turned to look out of the window.

After a moment of silence, the headmaster seemed to remember they were there. "Yes, I suppose we can start with you talking to Mr. Xander. I will go through the contact numbers I have for the parents of year eight students. I'll check and see whether they'll give permission for their children to speak with you."

DI Tyler nodded. "That will be very helpful, thank you. We'd also appreciate having a member of staff there during the questioning, a responsible adult looking after the child's interest."

The headmaster nodded and reached out for the telephone. "Yes, I'll organise that. I'll call Mr. Xander."

CHAPTER TEN

DC COLLINS WASN'T HAVING MUCH luck. He'd questioned twenty students so far, but none of them had been able to give him any case-changing information. But he'd made notes diligently. You could never tell what information would end up being crucial to a case.

With the last pupil he'd interviewed, Collins really thought he'd been on to something. The kid was twitchy and kept looking at the ground, twisting his hands in his lap.

Collins had been certain he was hiding something. Unfortunately, the only thing the kid was nervous about was spilling the beans about Francis bringing cigarettes into school and handing them out for a pound each.

It wasn't surprising, he supposed. Francis may have only been twelve, but he was a big lad, which is why when his body was pulled from the Thames, the pathologist had thought they were looking at a boy in his mid to late teens.

It made it worse somehow. The kid hadn't even reached his teens before he had his life cruelly snatched away.

Sitting in front of Collins now was a young Asian girl with long, silky black hair called Farzana Patani. She sat in front of Collins with her back straight and her hands clasped in her lap. Unlike most of the children he had interviewed so far, Farzana's tie was neatly fastened and her shirt was tucked in.

She was very eager to help. But, unfortunately, she didn't know anything that *could* help.

Collins spent a few minutes asking Farzana about the last time she'd seen Francis, which had been on Friday, at lunchtime. She gave him information he'd already heard from other students: Francis had a skateboard, and most evenings after school, he could be found around the Towers Estate making ramps and doing jumps and tricks.

One thing all the children mentioned was that Francis had a close friend called Alfie Adebayo.

Collins thought if anyone knew anything about Francis's murder and disappearance it should be Alfie Adebayo. The only problem was no one could find him. The headmaster had called his aunt, who was Alfie's legal guardian, and asked for permission to question him at school. She'd given her permission, but that wasn't much good when they couldn't locate Alfie.

Collins drew a line under his notes on his notepad. "Okay, Farzana, thank you very much for your help."

Farzana looked at him. She seemed almost disappointed. "Oh, is that all? Is there nothing else you need to ask me?"

Collins leaned his elbows heavily on the table and rested his chin against his hand. "I don't think so. Unless there's something you can think of that might be important."

Farzana's forehead creased in concentration, as if she really wanted to help, but then she shook her head and said, "Sorry. I can't think of anything."

Collins sighed and leant back in his chair. "Thanks very much for your help," he said, and the teacher who had been sitting next to Collins during all the interviews led Farzana outside.

Collins stared down at his notes.

Nothing.

Surely one of them must have seen or heard something, but maybe it wasn't anything to do with his friends at school.

The techies back in the lab were going over Francis's home computer. He might have been in contact with someone online. Maybe that would generate some more leads.

Collins heard heavy footsteps behind him. He turned around and saw a burly man dressed in a pair of tracksuit bottoms and trainers. His biceps bulged beneath a tight, white crew neck t-shirt. He had his hands on the shoulders of a small boy whom he pushed forward.

"I'm Mr. Xander," the man said. "I'm the sports teacher, and this is Alfie Adebayo. He was good friends with Francis, so I think he'll be able to help, won't you, Alfie?"

He pushed the little boy forward, and Collins turned his attention to the kid, who was obviously terrified.

"Thank you," Collins said. "Come and sit down opposite me, Alfie. There's nothing to worry about. I've only got a few questions. Nobody's going to get in any trouble."

Alfie took a few tentative steps forward and looked at the chair in front of Collins as if it were the last place on earth he wanted to be.

Why was the boy so scared? Did he know something?

Collins leaned forward resting his elbows on his knees so he could be on eye level with Alfie.

Alfie perched on the edge of the chair and looked nervously behind him at Mr. Xander.

"You won't get in trouble," Mr. Xander said in a deep rolling voice. "But you need to tell the truth Alfie, do you understand?"

To Collins's ears the voice seemed to hold the promise of a threat. He looked up sharply, but William Xander was smiling.

"Alfie," Collins said, trying to get the boy's attention on him and not the PE teacher. "I've heard you were good friends with Francis. Did you see him after school sometimes?"

Alfie waited a moment before answering, as if he were considering his response, then he gave a little nod.

"Speak up, boy." The PE teacher strode forward and prodded Alfie on the shoulder.

Collins looked up, annoyed. "Please," he said and held up a hand. "I'm sure Alfie is quite able to answer the questions."

"What sort of things did you used to do with Francis, Alfie?"

Alfie gave a shrug. "Just stuff. Hanging around, riding on skateboards, mostly."

Collins smiled. "You have a skateboard?"

It seemed to be the wrong thing to say. Alfie's face clouded over.

"No, we used to play with Francis's board." He sniffed. "He had a new one. A good board."

"And what about on Friday? Did you see Francis then?"

Alfie looked behind him at Mr. Xander again. "It's all right Alfie you can just look at me and answer the questions," Collins said, getting annoyed and wishing he could dismiss the PE teacher.

"I saw him for a little while on Friday," Alfie said.

"Okay, and what time did you see him?" Collins picked up his pen to make a note of the time.

"We played on the skateboard after school for a bit," Alfie said. "Then we both went home."

"What time did you go home, Alfie?"

Alfie shrugged.

"Answer the question, Alfie," Mr. Xander said, interrupting again.

"Dunno exactly, but I was back home before half-five."

"And do you know whether Francis was worried about anything? Anything bothering him? You can tell me. You won't get in any trouble, Alfie. We just want to find out who did this to him."

Alfie swallowed, and he was silent for so long that Collins thought he wouldn't reply. Eventually, Alfie licked his lips and then said something that Collins wasn't expecting.

"Are you sure it was Francis? Could it have been a mistake?"

Collins shook his head slowly. "No, Alfie. It wasn't a mistake."

"What happened to him? People have been saying stuff, but…"

"We're trying to find out exactly what happened to him. We need to find out who hurt him. Is there anything you can tell me that might help?"

Alfie vigorously shook his head. "No. I don't know anything."

"Maybe it's something you don't think is important. Perhaps Francis said something to you, or told you he was scared of someone."

Alfie bit down on his lip, then said, "No, Francis wasn't scared of anyone."

Collins tried to weigh up his next question. However he tried to sugarcoat it, it didn't sound any better.

"Alfie, can you tell me if Francis was happy at home?"

"I guess so."

"He wasn't having arguments with his mum and dad, or having any problems?"

Alfie shook his head. "No."

Collins felt bad for asking the question, but he had to do it. In the majority of murder cases, the murder wasn't carried out by a stranger. It usually involved somebody in the immediate family. Of course, the wooden disc in the boy's mouth and the wounds on his back didn't suggest family involvement. But Collins had heard of cases where familial killers had covered their tracks well, trying to divert attention.

After a few more questions, Collins nodded. "Thanks, Alfie. You've been a great help. If you think of anything else later, you can tell Mr. Xander here, or your aunt and they'll get in touch with me. And don't worry. You won't get into trouble if you've forgotten something. We just want to find out who did this to Francis. Do you understand?"

But Alfie was already out of the chair and reaching for his rucksack.

"Can I go now?"

Collins nodded, and Alfie Adebayo darted from the room.

CHAPTER ELEVEN

MACKINNON HEADED BACK TO DEREK'S house. He left half of the team working late into the night. He'd be among those that had to get to the station early tomorrow, so he needed to get home and get some much needed sleep.

Just two months ago, Derek had moved into a small three-bedroom house. It was just around the corner from his old place, but the rooms were bigger, and it meant Mackinnon didn't have to share his bedroom with boxes of old junk Derek was trying to sell.

Mackinnon got off the tube a stop early and decided to walk the rest of the way. He made a quick detour to the supermarket. He couldn't have curry *again*.

After grabbing a few things for dinner, he queued in the *'ten items or less lane,'* which somehow seemed to take longer than the regular checkouts. There were a few of those new self-service tills, but Mackinnon didn't trust them. Every time he'd tried them, something had gone wrong.

After finally handing over cash for the groceries, Mackinnon pulled out his mobile and called Chloe, listening to her describe her day as he walked the rest of the way. There was something nice about listening to her describe her day. A nice *normal* day with no murders.

But Chloe's day wasn't without stress. Chloe was in a panic trying to arrange a birthday party for her youngest daughter, Katy. Apparently Katy had informed Chloe, at the last minute, that she wanted a Halloween-themed party, complete with fancy dress, fake spiders and cobwebs.

Of course, as it was only a couple of days to Halloween the fancy dress shops had only a short supply of costumes and decorations.

He promised Chloe he'd do his best to get back on Wednesday for Katy's party. But it really all depended on how this case went. It was possible they might have a breakthrough before Wednesday. You never knew where or when a lead would turn up.

Mackinnon climbed the steps to Derek's front door and let himself in with his key.

"Derek," he called out.

There was no noise in the house. When Derek was home, the television was normally on.

No Derek yet, only Molly, bounding towards him.

He reached down to scratch behind the dog's ears. "Looks like it's just you and me tonight, Molly."

Mackinnon straightened up and started to walk towards the kitchen. "Let's see if Derek's left me a note."

Derek had indeed left a note. He was going to be staying at Julie's again tonight, and asked if Mackinnon would mind feeding Molly. Her dinner, apparently, was in the fridge.

Mackinnon glanced at the clock. "Sorry, sweetheart," he said to the dog. "You've had to wait a long time for your dinner tonight. I guess Derek didn't expect me to be home so late."

Inside the refrigerator, he found Molly's dinner complete with another note from Derek, which gave a detailed list of instructions.

Number one on the list was a request for Mackinnon to get Molly's food out of the fridge at least one hour before she ate. According to Derek, Molly didn't like eating cold food. It had to be room temperature.

Mackinnon glanced at Molly and then back at the note. "He can't be serious. I can't make you wait another hour for dinner."

He ignored Derek's note and unwrapped the food, peeling back the cling film that had been covering Molly's bowl.

He put it on the kitchen floor, and Molly tucked in straight away. She didn't seem to notice the temperature.

Mackinnon washed his hands and reached for the supermarket bag he'd left on the counter.

By the time he had finished pulling out the sliced chicken and the packet of stir-fry vegetables, Molly had finished her dinner.

She wandered over to the wall where her lead hung on a hook. She sat there patiently gazing back at him.

Mackinnon shook his head. "I'm not going out tonight. No curry."

Was it bad that Molly always expected him to take her for a walk, ending at the Indian takeaway down the street?

He turned his attention back to the plastic carrier bag and pulled out soy sauce, an onion, garlic and ginger.

As he rustled around in the cupboards, trying to locate a frying pan or wok, Molly stared at him with her big brown eyes, seemingly confused.

"I know this is different, but I have to make an effort to be a bit healthier. No more Indian takeaways. At least, not as many takeaways."

Mackinnon poured a little oil into the pan and quickly chopped up some onions followed by the chicken.

He dumped them into the sizzling pan, and tried to smother a yawn with the back of his hand. He didn't want to think about having to get up so early tomorrow morning.

The commuting was taking its toll. He couldn't imagine what it would be like if he didn't have Derek's place to crash in during the week.

As Mackinnon cooked, Molly wandered back over to him and sat by his heels, gazing upwards, seemingly more and more confused.

Mackinnon supposed it was because she had never actually seen him cook before.

After he finished dinner, Mackinnon took Molly down into the garden, and let her run around for a bit.

After ten minutes of playing catch with Molly's red rubber ball, Mackinnon sat down on the back steps and watched his breath as it produced steamy white puffs. He felt a familiar burning in his chest. That would teach him to play with Molly so soon after eating.

He thought about what the team would be doing tonight, and how they would methodically be going through the background of Francis Eze's parents. The techies would be combing through Francis's computer, trying to find something that might indicate who killed the boy.

It was possible that Mackinnon could turn up tomorrow and find that the team had unearthed a wealth of new information. They could be hot on the heels of Francis Eze's killer.

He hoped so.

CHAPTER TWELVE

ALFIE SAT HUDDLED UP IN one corner of the sofa. He would have preferred to have been in his bedroom, but his aunt said she wanted him where she could see him, so he didn't get up to any mischief.

It wouldn't be long now before his uncle came home, and Alfie was dreading it.

His aunt had noticed the time as well. She'd removed her great big, dangly, gold earrings and was sitting on the sofa next to Alfie with a makeup remover wipe, scrubbing lipstick and eye makeup off her face.

Alfie's uncle didn't like makeup.

He called it the Devil's paint. His aunt seemed to like it, though. During the day, she always wore lashings of mascara and the brightest pink lipstick. But every night before Alfie's uncle was due home from work, she would wipe it all off and leave her face shiny and bare.

They were supposed to be watching TV together. The

TV was droning on and pictures were flashing on the screen, but Alfie wasn't really paying attention. He was still thinking about Francis and Mr. X.

But no matter how long Alfie thought about it and tried to work it out, he couldn't see a way out of this mess.

He wasn't even safe at home. If his aunt knew what had happened she would be quick to hand him over to Mr. X.

Alfie wished he'd never come here. He sat forward on the sofa and turned to his aunt. "Think I'll go to bed," he said.

His aunt turned to him with narrowed eyes and said, "You haven't had any dinner yet."

Alfie put a hand against his stomach. "I'm not feeling very well."

Aunt Erika grunted and nodded.

Alfie stood up and skirted round her feet, heading for his bedroom.

There were three bedrooms in this flat. His aunt and uncle shared one, Alfie had the smallest, which was a little box room. Alfie had been told not to go into the third room.

The room was for his Aunt Erika's visitors. People who came to ask favours of Mr. X. They knew Alfie's aunt was the one to speak to if they needed help from the spirits.

Alfie shivered as he passed the room.

His aunt and uncle were wrong. Alfie wasn't evil, but there was definitely evil in that room.

Alfie put his pyjamas on and got into bed, he couldn't be bothered to have a wash or clean his teeth. When he was at his grandma's, she used to check on him every night. She would come into his room to make sure he'd cleaned his teeth and said his prayers. But his aunt didn't seem to bother about things like that.

Thinking of his grandmother made Alfie feel homesick. He wondered what she was doing in Southend-on-Sea with his little brother Mickey. He pictured them sitting round a table eating big bowls of domoda, his grandma called it her special peanut stew.

It hadn't really been that long since Alfie had seen them. But it seemed like forever. It was all Mickey's fault that his grandma hadn't let Alfie go to Southend with them. He was the one who always used to get into trouble, and Alfie used to have to help him out.

Mickey loved to mouth off at the bigger boys. He was good at that. Then once he'd got them worked up and showing their fists, Mickey would come running to Alfie for help, and Alfie would have to stick up for his little brother.

Of course, his grandmother didn't listen when Alfie tried to explain. Nobody ever thought Mickey could possibly do anything wrong. With his cute dimpled cheeks and his shiny brown eyes, everyone thought he was a little angel. So Alfie always got the blame, and his grandmother said she was too old to deal with such a naughty little boy like Alfie.

So she'd moved to Southend-on-Sea and taken her little angel, Mickey, with her and left Alfie, the naughty one, with his aunt and uncle.

For as long as he could remember, his grandma had always said Alfie had bad blood. His mother had run away from home at sixteen. According to his grandma, Alfie's mother drank too much and one morning, when Alfie was only four years old, she'd drunk so much rum that it killed her.

His grandma said that was when she'd been saddled with them, and she reminded Alfie and Mickey at every opportunity, how lucky they were. If their grandma hadn't taken them in, they would have gone into care.

At the time, Alfie hadn't known what 'care' was, but he was pretty sure he didn't want to find out.

Alfie turned over in bed and buried his face in his pillow. Surely if he went to his grandma now, she wouldn't turn him away, not if he told her what had happened to Francis.

Alfie wrapped the duvet tightly around him. Would she believe him, though?

Would anyone believe him?

CHAPTER THIRTEEN

EVERYBODY HATED MONDAY MORNINGS, IT went without saying, but in Rachel Dawson's opinion, Tuesday was the worst day of the week.

Tuesdays were her least favourite because they ran a special offer at lunchtime—two for the price of one—which meant the restaurant would be absolutely packed.

She used to love working here when the restaurant had been run by Jon Santorini, but he'd retired last year and the new owners didn't run the business in the same way. They were hardly ever here, so the staff took advantage.

Rachel was the first one at the restaurant today, which wasn't unusual. Sometimes, Victor, the daytime chef surprised her by turning up early, but more often than not he was over thirty minutes late.

Rachel thrust the key into the lock, opened the front door and pressed her finger on the large, red button just inside the entrance to open the shutters.

She wouldn't have minded if the pay had been a little higher, but on Tuesdays the restaurant was packed out with customers who only came for the special offers, and those kinds of customers usually didn't leave tips, so Rachel was paid the same money as every other day in the week, despite running herself ragged on the restaurant floor.

When she got to the restaurant's kitchen, Rachel swore.

"Bastards," she muttered.

She usually liked the early shifts. It suited her to be finished for the day by three o'clock, so she could collect her son from school, but she was getting majorly pissed off with the staff who worked the evening shifts.

Rachel scowled at the stainless steel counters in the kitchen. They were scattered with crumbs and, what looked like fragments of chopped onions. The usually shiny steel surface had been smeared where someone had quickly run a dirty dishcloth over the work surfaces rather than clean them properly.

She didn't have time to clean up their mess. Soon Santorini's early morning customers would be lining up for their coffee and croissants.

Rachel swore again when she saw the overflowing bin.

She chucked her handbag onto the counter and took the huge ring of keys from the hook by the refrigerator. She selected the key for the back door.

She unlocked the door, pulling it wide, letting the early morning mist and cold air into the kitchen.

She shivered and lifted the lid of the bin. Rachel wrinkled her nose as the smell of fish wafted up towards her.

Why couldn't they have just emptied this last night? Last night it wouldn't have smelled so bad.

She yanked up the black, plastic sack and swore again as it caught on the side of the bin and ripped a little.

This was turning into a really bad day. She sighed and glanced up at the clock, wondering how long it would be before Victor turned up for his shift. He was supposed to be at the restaurant early on Tuesdays to start his prep.

You just couldn't get well-trained staff these days, not reliable ones anyway. Rachel heaved the black bag out of the bin, praying the bag wouldn't split.

She staggered to the back door with it, heaved it over the step, carried it out into the small alleyway behind the row of shops and walked towards the communal bins. The heavy sack bashed her shins with each step. She hoped it wasn't leaking.

The shops on this stretch shared four large metal bins with fold-over lids. Rachel dumped the bag by the foot of the bin and then jumped as she saw a movement.

She yelped and stepped backwards. Her cheeks flushed when she realised that it was only a marmalade-coloured cat that liked to haunt the alleyway, looking for scraps.

She breathed out a sigh of relief. She didn't mind the cat. A couple of months ago, she had seen a huge, grey rat out here, and ever since, she'd been a bit wary.

She moved forward again and picked up the lid of the bin, yanking it upwards. It always seemed to get stuck half-way, but another firm shove did the trick, and the bin clattered open.

At first, Rachel didn't register anything was wrong.

On instinct, she leaned down to pick up the bag of restaurant waste, then she hesitated. She straightened up, raised herself up on tiptoes and peered into the large bin.

Just a man's shoe, she told herself. People were always dumping their rubbish in the restaurant's bin.

She leaned a little closer. A brown paper McDonald's bag covered most of the shoe. Rachel reached in and pulled it out of the way.

Attached to the shoe, covered in curly black hair, was a human leg.

Rachel dropped the McDonald's bag and staggered backwards. She put a hand to her mouth as she felt the bile rise in her throat.

The bag of rubbish forgotten, she ran towards the back door of the restaurant and staggered inside the kitchen.

Victor, the chef, had finally arrived.

The kitchen smelled of lemons. Victor was busy squirting the counters with disinfectant.

"It's a bloody state," he said. "I can't believe they left it like this knowing we would have to clean it up. I'm going to have to have a word with them. It can't go on like this."

When Rachel didn't reply, he turned. "What's wrong with you?"

For a moment, Rachel couldn't find the words. She pointed behind her to the door. "I think... I saw..."

She couldn't get the words out. She took a deep breath.

"I just saw something really horrible in the bin."

Victor frowned. "Another rat? Well, it's not surprising. Bins are like a magnet to them. You can't get rid of rats. Not really they always come back. Did you know in London you're never more than a couple of metres from a rat?" He grinned. "I heard that there are more rats in London than there are people!"

He turned and continued spraying the counters.

"Victor, I'm serious…"

Victor set down the lemon-scented disinfectant. "Is this your way of getting out of emptying the bin?"

Rachel shook her head. "No, really, I saw… I mean, I think I saw…"

She blinked. *Had she really seen it? Had it been her imagination?* The way the rubbish was all piled up in there, it could have been a mistake. Maybe it wasn't what she thought it had been.

"Please, Victor," she said. "Can you just come and look?"

Victor wiped his hands on a towel and followed her outside.

"All right. But hurry up. I've got loads to do this morning."

They walked towards the communal bins, and Rachel nodded towards the one in the middle. "It's that one. There's something in it."

She felt all the hairs on the back of her neck stand up as Victor reached for the lid.

He didn't seem quite so confident now. He stood as far away as he could, with just one hand on the lid, lifting the metal inch by inch.

The lid creaked upwards. The tip of Victor's tongue poked out between his teeth as he concentrated.

Rachel looked away. She didn't want to see it again.

"Shit," Victor said.

And Rachel knew she'd been right. She hadn't imagined anything.

There was a body in the bin.

CHAPTER FOURTEEN

WHEN MACKINNON GOT TO THE scene behind Santorini's restaurant it was already packed with police and SOCOs.

The pathologist was leaning over the body.

Mackinnon pulled up the collar of his coat as he walked towards the melee. The alley behind the restaurant was a wind trap. The wind whistled past and made an eerie crooning sound.

The crime scene photographers were already finishing up, and DI Tyler was standing close to the pathologist, frowning down at him. After putting on shoe covers, Mackinnon made his way forward.

Mackinnon had already been given the details. But no matter how carefully the scene was described beforehand, it never prepared him for seeing something like this.

On the floor by the pathologist's feet, was a young black male.

The victim was still wearing jeans, but his t-shirt had been ripped in two. On his back, the symbol X had been carved into his flesh. The red slashes ran from the man's shoulder to hip bone on both sides.

Mackinnon swallowed. Despite the horror of the scene, one of the first things Mackinnon noticed was the lack of blood. The victim had been killed elsewhere and dumped.

"Not pretty is it?" DI Tyler said.

"How long do you think he's been there?" Mackinnon asked.

Tyler paused and looked down at the pathologist. "We don't know yet. He was dumped in the bin. We've only just got him out. Lovely job for the SOCOs."

Mackinnon looked up and saw SOCO officers routing through, labelling and photographing various items from the rubbish. Mackinnon didn't envy them that. It stank enough from where he was standing.

"We know he was obviously killed somewhere else then dumped in the bin. The pathologist believes he was killed three to four days ago. But as for how long he's been in the bin? That's anyone's guess."

"So he was killed around the same time as Francis Eze," Mackinnon said.

Tyler nodded. "Yes, and the same cross carved into the poor bloke's back, too."

Tyler turned to walk away. "Christ, I need a fag," he said.

Mackinnon followed Tyler. "How old is he, do you think?"

Tyler shook his head. "There's no ID on him, but I reckon we are looking at a man in his early twenties."

"Not another kid then."

Tyler shook his head. "No, the pathologist thinks not."

"That's something at least."

Tyler pulled a face and pulled out a packet of cigarettes, as they ducked under the police tape.

Mackinnon looked around the alley as they walked. "No cameras around here?"

DI Tyler shook his head. "Not around here, they've got some at the front of the restaurant and some in that side road over there." He nodded towards the alleyway's exit. "We might get lucky, I suppose. I don't like our chances, though."

They were far enough away now for Tyler to light his cigarette. He leaned back against a squad car and extracted a cigarette from the packet.

"DC Webb's looking through mispers to see if anyone's reported the poor guy missing."

A shout attracted their attention. The uniformed PC standing by the tape waved to them.

Tyler gave a tight smile. "How much do you want to bet that our eminent pathologist has found a lovely wooden disc in our victim's mouth?"

Not much, Mackinnon thought. He thought the odds were strongly in Tyler's favour.

As they approached the scene, the pathologist waved them over. He was a short man with thinning grey hair and quite a large paunch. He squatted over the body with a grunt.

"I thought this might interest you," the pathologist said. And with one gloved hand, he poked a finger into the victim's mouth.

"Another pouch?" Tyler leaned closer.

"Yes," the pathologist said. He pulled a small, red pouch from the victim's mouth. It was sticky with partially dried saliva.

After one of the crime scene photographers had captured enough images, Tyler snapped on a pair of blue latex gloves and loosened the top of the pouch.

"Bingo," he said, with a face like thunder as he looked down at the small wooden disc. "Smooth on one side, and a cross on the other."

They put the wooden disc and the pouch into a plastic evidence bag, and Tyler began to peel off his gloves. Mackinnon turned to walk away.

"Wait a minute," the pathologist said. "That wasn't the only thing I wanted you to see."

"It wasn't?" Tyler asked, frowning. "What else have you got for us?"

The pathologist's gloved finger curled back the upper lip of the victim. "See this." He exposed the man's teeth. They appeared to be encased in some kind of golden metal.

"He's wearing a brace," Mackinnon said.

"It's not a brace. It's one of those grill things," Tyler said.

"Yes," the pathologist said. "They are becoming more popular."

Mackinnon nodded. He remembered seeing them on rap stars and pop stars. One of Sarah's magazines had had a picture of Katy Perry, beaming with a mouth full of metal, on the front cover.

"They're meant for decoration, not for straightening teeth," Tyler said. "It depends on how many people have this kind of grill, but it might help us narrow down who our victim is."

Tyler nodded at the pathologist. "Thanks, Doc."

Tyler strode away and Mackinnon followed. "I'll get Collins onto that. He can track down some dentists in the area. You never know, we might get lucky."

Mackinnon nodded, and as Tyler went off to ring Collins, he turned back to look at the victim. All around him the buildings loomed over them, grey and ugly. A light rain began to fall.

In one of the flats above Santorini's restaurant Mackinnon could see a floppy witch's hat on the window sill. The window had been covered with spray-on cobwebs, the kind Katy had wanted for her party.

He never understood the obsession with the macabre some people had. He saw enough real life horror stories in this line of work.

CHAPTER FIFTEEN

COLLINS WAS DRIVING TO WORK and had to use hands-free when he got the call from DI Tyler. It had taken him two attempts to connect it. According to the instructions, his phone was supposed to seamlessly connect to the Peugeot's stereo system via Bluetooth, but in Collins's opinion, there was nothing seamless about it. The bloody thing hardly ever worked.

He assured the detective inspector he'd investigate the grills and look into any dentists in the area who fitted them as soon as he got to the station.

The daily commute into the city from Essex was killing him. But what could he do? He and Debra had two kids now, and there was no way he could afford anything in central London.

Just five minutes after the call from DI Tyler, Evie Charlesworth from Wood Street Station rang. This time

Collins didn't bother trying the hands-free. He stopped the car in front of a betting shop and answered the call.

He'd pulled up too close to the bus stop, so he kept an eagle eye on the rearview mirror to make sure he wasn't in the way of any approaching buses.

Evie had already done most of the legwork for him and gave him the address of a dentist.

"Evie, you're an angel," Collins said.

"So I've been told," Evie said dryly. "We've found a logo carved into the back of the grill. It's small, but it's possible to see the letters H and S. I'm guessing it stands for Hollywood Smiles. It's one of the biggest and most well-known dentists in the area, and they make these kinds of grills. If we're lucky, he might have the victim on record."

Evie recited the address, and Collins thanked her, hung up, and used Google maps to locate the dental surgery.

He performed a U-turn and headed off to find Hollywood Smiles. It only took him ten minutes.

Finding a space to park, however, was not so easy.

Collins crawled around the back streets, looking for a parking space. He eventually settled for one in front of a bin, next to a kebab shop. He wasn't sure if it was a legitimate parking space, but it would have to do. Hopefully this wouldn't take long.

He headed back to the dentist, pulling his jacket tightly around him. The October chill had definitely set in now, after a mild September.

The dentist's surgery stood out amongst the row of shops. The outside was painted bright white and the sign over the large front windows was blue-and-white. It gave the surgery a clean, sterile appearance.

As Collins entered, the bell above the door rang. A young woman, with her auburn hair tied tightly in a bun, sat behind a white desk. She looked up and smiled at him.

Collins noticed that, although her gleaming teeth were an unnatural shade of white, she wasn't wearing a grill.

Collins pulled out his ID and introduced himself. As soon as the woman realised he wasn't a customer, the bright smile dropped from her face.

She pursed her lips, then said, "Well, we have two dentists working here. Which one do you want to speak to?"

Collins had no idea. He smiled at her. "Both of them."

She picked up the phone on her desk and thumped in four numbers. "Dr. McGuire? Yes, there's a policeman out here. He wants to speak to you… Yes, that's right, a policeman." She hung up the phone. "He won't be a moment. If you'd like to take a seat?"

Collins put his hands in his pockets, and decided no, he wouldn't like to take a seat. They were all just hard back chairs and looked pretty uncomfortable. Besides, he'd been sitting down in his car since he left Essex at six o'clock this morning.

The dentist didn't take long to arrive.

He came out into the reception area, looking very worried. He completely ignored the receptionist and walked towards Collins.

"Police?" The dentist raised his eyebrows. "I'm not sure how I can help you."

Collins showed his ID again and tried to reassure him that he just needed some help with an enquiry.

"You're Dr. McGuire?"

"That's right," the dentist said. "I'm one of only two dentists who work here full-time, though we have five others who work on a part-time basis."

"Do you fit grills?" Collins asked.

"Ah, yes." The dentist seemed to relax now that he was on familiar territory. "It is my specialty."

"We're trying to identify a murder victim. He was wearing a grill, which we think was made by your dental surgery. It had a logo of an H and S in a circle, just like yours." Collins nodded at the poster above the reception desk.

Dr. McGuire nodded. "Well, of course, I'll try to be as much help as I can, but the grills aren't actually made here. We just take a cast of the patient's teeth. The casts are sent away, and the grills are made off site. It typically takes a couple of weeks for the grills to be produced. When they come back, we call the patient to come in for a fitting. If there are any problems, we make changes to the grill. So it takes a long time. Of course, there are some cowboys out there. Some people set up on their own without any dental qualifications… That can lead to all sorts of problems, teeth grinding, ulcers—"

Collins interrupted. "Very interesting. But I would like to know if you would recognise the grill?"

The dentist nodded. "Ah, I see. It depends on the type, but if it is our high-end stuff, I would. They are unique, and I do keep records, photographic records actually, of each grill that we've made. Not for this type of thing, obviously. I wanted to use the photographs for a brochure. So patients can flick through and decide which grill they'd like to have."

Dr. McGuire got to his feet and walked across to the reception desk. He said a few words in a hushed tone to the receptionist, who leaned under the desk and pulled out a file.

"I'm sorry about having to talk out here," Dr. McGuire said to Collins. "But we don't really have an office area, and my dental nurse is prepping for the next patient."

Collins nodded. "It's fine. I'm sorry to disturb you at work. Hopefully we can get this done quickly, and you can get back to your patients."

The dentist nodded and opened up the file. "I don't suppose you know when he would have had the grill fitted?"

Collins shook its head. "I'm afraid not."

"Can you describe it?"

"I can do better than that," Collins said and pulled out his mobile phone. He scrolled through the photo app until he found the photograph of the grill that Evie had forwarded to him.

He showed the display to the dentist. "Do you recognise it?"

The dentist pulled it towards him. "I see, yes. It's a gold base, so not one of our top end grills. The top end ones of course are made of platinum. But there is something... Yes, this is interesting. Most people prefer diamonds, but I see this one is a ruby," he said, pointing at a tiny speck to the right of the grill.

"Yes, I'm not sure it's unique," he said. "If I recall correctly, I've done a couple of those. Just a moment."

Dr. McGuire started to flick through the pages of the file.

"Here we are," he said. "Yes, that's right. It's this one. It wasn't that long ago—only six months."

Collins took the file the dentist offered, and compared the two images. The one on his phone and the blown up image the dentist had shown him did look very similar.

"Are you sure it's the same one?"

"Oh, yes. It's an art, you see, this type of work. Far more interesting than tooth whitening and fillings," he said.

Collins allowed himself to feel a spark of hope. "Does that mean you'll have this on file? You'll have the patient's details?"

The dentist nodded. "We should have. It's got a reference number. I just need to check that against the spreadsheet of patient references on the computer. I won't be a moment."

The dentist left Collins sitting on a hard plastic chair and headed off to check the computer.

For want of anything better to do, Collins picked up one of the flyers on the table. It offered twenty percent off tooth whitening for the rest of October.

Less than two minutes later, Dr. McGuire returned with a huge grin on his face.

"Excellent, we have him on record," he said. "I don't suppose I should really be sharing patients' records... But as it's a murder investigation no doubt you could get a warrant anyway."

Collins nodded. "Exactly."

The dentist shrugged and handed Collins the printout. "That's the name we have on file. Adam Jonah. And his address. Of course, that would have been six months ago, but hopefully it's up to date."

"Excellent," Collins said. "Thanks very much for your help." He nodded at the dentist and started to walk towards the door.

"Oh before you go," Dr. McGuire said, "we do have an offer on at the moment. I guess you're not really a grill man, are you?"

Collins shook his head.

"No, I thought not. But there is twenty percent off on tooth whitening this month," Dr. McGuire said, waggling the flyer.

"No, thanks," Collins said and closed the door behind him.

He couldn't believe putting bleach on teeth did them any good, and he was perfectly happy with his own slightly off-white colour.

CHAPTER SIXTEEN

AS SOON AS COLLINS HAD phoned the station and given them the name and address of Adam Jonah, Tyler had put in a request for a warrant.

A few hours later, a small team of officers, including DC Collins and DI Tyler, gathered outside forty-two, Herring Lane, Poplar.

One of the uniformed officers hammered on the door. They weren't really expecting an answer, and they were surprised when a young man answered the door.

He'd clearly only just got out of bed. His frizzy hair stood on end. He blinked as he stood there barefoot and bare-chested.

He wore a pair of navy tracksuit bottoms several sizes too big for him, and he had to keep one hand clamped on the waistband, holding them up.

"What's this all about?" he demanded to know.

He was shown the warrant, and he stood aside to let the officers in, but not without making a hell of a lot of noise as he did so.

"You can't just come in here. You've got no reason to break in here like this. This is my home."

DI Tyler turned to him. "You live here?" The man hesitated, then nodded. "And your name?"

The man chewed on his lower lip as his eyes darted right then left.

Tyler crossed his arms over his chest. "It's not a difficult question."

The man rolled his eyes. "It's Kofi. Kofi Ayensu."

"Well, Kofi, do you know a man called Adam Jonah?"

Kofi hesitated, then said, "Why? What's he done?"

"I'd appreciate it if you answered the question, Kofi. I don't like my questions being answered with questions," DI Tyler said. "You'll find this will go a lot easier if you cooperate."

"I am cooperating," Kofi said. "Hang on. What are they doing?"

He pointed at two uniformed officers who were stripping his bed.

Tyler didn't answer. "Did you know Adam Jonah?"

Kofi nodded. "Yeah, of course I do. We share the flat." He hesitated. "Hang on, why did you say *did* I know him?"

His head whipped around taking in all the officers in his flat. Everyone was busy searching cupboards and pulling out drawers. Nobody paid him any attention.

"He's all right, isn't he? Adam?" Kofi asked.

"When did you last see him?"

"A few days back," Kofi said. "But that's not unusual. I work nightshifts, he works days. Often we don't see each other for days at a time."

Kofi walked away from Tyler and moved through the bedroom doorway. "I don't understand what's going on. What's happened to Adam?"

"We believe Adam has been killed," Tyler said, watching Kofi closely for his reaction.

Kofi's eyes widened, and he shook his head. "No, not Adam." He ran a hand through his frizzy hair. "Are you sure?"

"We think the body we found is Adam, but we'll need someone to identify the body. He's not been formally identified yet. We've been led to believe it is Adam from the grill he was wearing over his teeth."

Kofi's shoulders slumped. "He did wear a grill."

Kofi seemed to be about to say something else, when one of the uniformed officers called out to DI Tyler.

"Sir, I think you'll want to see this."

The officer pulled out a tray from under the bed.

DI Tyler walked towards him. His eyes focused on the objects on the tray.

After a moment, Tyler stopped and looked at Kofi. "Are these yours?"

"So what? Hey, there's nothing wrong with that."

Tyler raised an eyebrow, then looked back at the collection the uniformed officer was now cataloguing.

A red cloth lined the tray, and on the cloth, there was a bowl and several white candles.

What looked like a ball of hair was crammed in beside the candles.

But what interested Tyler most of all was the fact that the bowl was full to the brim with blood.

CHAPTER SEVENTEEN

"WHAT DO YOU THINK?" DI Tyler asked. "Do you think he did it?"

DI Tyler and Mackinnon stood in the darkened room, staring at Kofi Ayensu through the one-way glass.

Kofi Ayensu stared back. He couldn't see them, but he knew they were there.

Kofi would only be able to see his reflection. The one-way mirror had a reflective coating applied in a very thin layer.

The only reason Kofi Ayensu couldn't see them was because the room he was sitting in was very brightly lit, so there was plenty of light reflected back from the mirror's surface.

In the room behind the mirror, where Tyler and Mackinnon stood, the glass acted as a window. With the lights dimmed in the viewing room, very little light was reflected, so they had a perfect view of Kofi, fidgeting and chewing on his nails.

Mackinnon exhaled. "I don't think he did it. I mean, he'd be some kind of fool to keep the blood laying around if he did. And the flat is definitely not the scene of the murder. The SOCOs have turned the place inside out. There were small areas of blood and a little bit of blood splatter, but nowhere near the amount we would have found if he had killed Adam Jonah there."

Tyler nodded. "True, but he could have killed him somewhere else, and brought the blood back." Tyler shrugged. "Maybe as a sick souvenir?"

Mackinnon didn't think so. But it was one of those gut feelings that he couldn't really explain, and definitely not something that he could rely on when preparing evidence.

"Okay," Tyler said, running a hand through his grey hair. "I'm going to go back in. I'll take DC Webb in with me this time." Tyler glanced at his watch. "Round two."

Mackinnon stayed where he was, ready to observe the interview.

He checked his mobile and saw a missed call from Chloe. He quickly typed a text, promising to call her soon.

A moment later, he saw DI Tyler entering the interview room followed by DC Webb.

As soon as the door opened, Kofi's head sprang up, and he slapped his palms flat on the table.

"This is racism," he said. "It's just stupid. I would never have hurt Adam. I don't know what to say to make you believe me, but when I get out of here, I'm gonna find myself a lawyer. That's right." He crossed his arms over his chest and nodded. "Uh-huh. I'm going to get lawyered up, then you better watch your step. This is racism, pure and simple."

Tyler didn't react. He set down the paperwork, pulled out a chair and sat down. DC Webb did the same and they introduced themselves for the purpose of the tape.

Kofi groaned, leaning back in his chair.

"It doesn't look very good for you, Kofi," DI Tyler said. "Your flatmate has been murdered, and you didn't even notice he was missing. We've found evidence at your flat, including a bowl of blood."

"I already explained that," Kofi said. "We work different shifts. We often don't see each other for days."

Kofi's shoulders slumped. "You've got to believe me. I wouldn't have hurt him. He was a friend. I've known him for years."

Kofi chewed on a fingernail. At this rate, he'd have none left. "Look, there was something a bit odd about Adam in the last week or so. He kept going on about how his luck was going to change, how he was going to meet a spirit guide called Mr. X, who had offered to help him."

Tyler smirked. "Mr. X? Really? You're going to have to do better than that, Kofi."

There was a knock at the door, and DI Tyler paused the tape then walked across the room to open the door.

Mackinnon couldn't see who it was from the viewing room, so he opened the door and stuck his head out into the corridor, just in time to see Collins standing there with a handful of papers.

Collins looked a little sheepish.

DI Tyler closed the interview room door behind him. "Shit! Are you sure?"

Collins nodded. "Yep, she said something about looking under a microscope and seeing nuclei or was it a nucleus? Not exactly sure on that bit. But anyway, she's one hundred percent positive the blood is from a bird, most likely a chicken."

Tyler shook his head. "So we don't have anything. We have nothing at all to link him to the murder. Apart from the fact they shared a flat."

Collins shook his head and took a step back. "No, I'm sorry, sir. The blood definitely wasn't human."

Tyler nodded, then headed back inside.

Mackinnon ducked back into the interview viewing room.

Kofi's eyes followed Tyler around the room, until he sat down.

"Talk to me, Kofi," Tyler said. "Convince me you are innocent."

"I shouldn't have to. It's only because my religion is different from yours. That's why you are suspicious. I was doing a purification ritual. I'm starting a new job soon. I needed the good luck.

"You think a purification ritual is weird? Well, what about all the Christian stuff? You know, drinking Christ's blood and eating parts of his body. That's pretty weird to somebody who's not Christian."

"It's nothing to do with religion, Kofi. We need to find out who killed Adam, and right now, the only suspect we've got is you."

Kofi shook his head vigorously. "No, that's not right. Why aren't you talking to his boss? They had a huge argument last week. He should be a suspect not me."

Tyler leaned forward in his chair, and Mackinnon straightened up. This was more like it.

Kofi saw the interest on DI Tyler's face.

He nodded eagerly. "Yeah, he had a huge argument with his boss, and he was sacked last week. It got physical," Kofi said and nodded. "He's the one you should be questioning.

"Adam told me his boss threatened him. He said if he saw Adam round there again, he'd kill him."

CHAPTER EIGHTEEN

ALFIE SAT AT THE TABLE with Aunt Erika and Uncle Remi. They sat in silence. The only sound was the ticking carriage clock on the mantelpiece.

Alfie's plate was covered with meat stew and mashed potatoes. He felt his stomach roll. He couldn't eat all this. He was never hungry anymore. But if he didn't eat that would make them angry.

Alfie looked up and saw his uncle staring at him with narrowed eyes. Alfie looked away.

Alfie reached for the salt and sprinkled it all over his mashed potatoes.

"Not so much salt," his aunt said. "Why do you need so much? You haven't even tasted it yet."

Alfie bit his lip.

"Sorry," he whispered.

He leaned forward to place the salt back on the table, but his elbow caught his glass of water.

It seemed to happen in slow motion. The glass tipped perilously for a moment before falling on its side and flooding the tablecloth.

Alfie's uncle exploded with rage. He stood up, yanked back his chair, which made a screeching sound against the tiles, and made a grab for Alfie.

Alfie ducked so quickly he fell off his chair. He crawled under the table.

"I'm sorry. I'm sorry. I'm sorry." He repeated the words over and over, clutching his knees to his chest.

"We need to sort the boy out," his uncle said. "This clumsiness isn't natural."

"No, no, no," Alfie said. "I'm sorry. I'm really sorry."

He saw Uncle Remi's face appear under the table, just a foot away, and Alfie yelped in fright.

He scooted back as far as he could, out of the big man's reach.

Uncle Remi stared at Alfie, then said, "There's evil in you, boy. I won't have you bringing evil into my house."

Aunt Erika spoke up. "It's okay, I'm in control."

For a moment, he thought she was going to tell Uncle Remi to leave him alone, to tell him that he didn't mean to knock the glass over.

But she didn't.

"I've spoken to Mr. X," Aunt Erika said. "He's going to do a cleansing ritual."

Alfie felt as though he'd been punched in the chest.

"No, no," he screamed.

This time Alfie wasn't scared of his uncle. Nothing

scared him as much as the thought of being handed over to Mr. X.

He exploded past them both, barrelling into Uncle Remi.

His uncle reared backwards into the cabinet. There was a crash as one of the glass cabinet doors smashed.

Alfie ran down the hallway. He could hear his uncle shouting after him, but he didn't stop. He wrenched open the front door and ran outside into the rain.

He didn't stop running until he'd reached Burdett Road on the other end of the Towers Estate.

He felt dizzy and sick and rested his hand on the rough brick wall, trying to get his breath back as the rain drenched his jumper and trickled down his neck.

He needed to do something. Who could he ask to help him? Someone in school? Mr. Xander?

Just thinking about the teacher sent chills up Alfie's spine. He couldn't ask him. He'd think it was all Alfie's fault.

Maybe he could go to the police. They had come to the school. The policeman Alfie had spoken to didn't seem too bad. Maybe he would listen.

Alfie shivered. He hadn't stopped to put on a coat and his jumper was wet through.

He saw a gang of kids he recognised from the year above him at school. They'd made some half-hearted effort to dress up for Halloween, even though it wasn't until Thursday.

They rushed from doorway to doorway, trying to avoid the rain. One of them wore a witch's hat. Another had a white sheet over him trying to look like a ghost. They were on their rounds, milking their opportunity to get sweets from the local residents. Halloween once a year obviously didn't get them enough treats.

Alfie carried on watching them as they moved from house to house. They ran away from one door, giggling when an old man waved his stick at them. Obviously there was one resident who was sick of Halloween already.

Alfie wished he was among the group of kids, messing about and laughing. They didn't have anything to worry about.

Last year he and Francis had gone around the estate knocking on doors, carrying a little plastic beach bucket to hold their stash of sweets. They'd taken Mickey with them, too.

But now Francis had gone, and Alfie didn't know if he'd ever see Mickey again.

Alfie swallowed. He didn't want to think about Francis. He didn't want to think how his friend had died, and he definitely didn't want to think how the last thought going through Francis's mind might have been to wonder why Alfie had left him.

CHAPTER NINETEEN

MACKINNON WAS STARTING TO FEEL the effects of his early start that morning. He couldn't stop yawning as he walked home from the tube station to Derek's.

He spied a group of kids trick or treating at the end of the road. There were still two days to Halloween, but they'd been at it all week.

He'd called his parents on the way home. They'd moved to a new house in Devon, and he hadn't made it down there to visit them yet. He felt bad, but with work and Chloe and the girls, time just seemed to slip away.

After he had heard all about his mother's new book club, she passed the phone over to Mackinnon's father for a few words.

As he rounded the corner and turned into Derek's road, he promised to visit them soon and ended the call.

Derek had said he was going to be home tonight, but Mackinnon couldn't see any lights on. He let himself in and heard the familiar commentary of an American football game.

Since Derek had bought Game Pass from the NFL, he hadn't missed a game this season.

Mackinnon had watched quite a few of the games too, and was finding it strangely addictive. The Game Pass stream even had the American adverts, which were very different from their English equivalents.

One day last week, in a five minute period, they had seen adverts for Viagra, baldness and a special comb that was supposed to brush hair and cut it at the same time. Mackinnon had no idea how that worked.

Mackinnon opened the front door, took his coat off, chucked it over the banisters and leaned down to greet Molly who seemed very glad he was back.

Derek got out of his chair as Mackinnon walked to the doorway of the living room.

Derek held up his empty bottle of beer. "You want one?"

Mackinnon nodded and followed Derek into the open plan kitchen area. Mackinnon thought this was one of the main reasons Derek had bought the house. He could walk to the kitchen and fix dinner or grab a beer out of the fridge without missing a second of his precious American football.

"Who's playing?" Mackinnon asked.

"Seahawks vs. the Rams. It's a re-run of the Monday night game. Seahawks are looking pretty good so far."

Mackinnon watched as one of the Seahawks snatched the ball and ran up the field like lightning. As he got closer to the goal line, he turned to the defender chasing him, gripped the ball in one hand and waved with the other.

"Did you see that? Was he really waving at the defender?"

Derek watched the replay. "He only just made it, too. I imagine someone will have words with him about that. The NFL doesn't like taunting."

"The coach won't be too happy either. That distraction almost cost them the touchdown."

"He'll probably get a fine," Derek said. "I've got tickets to the NFL game at Wembley on Saturday. It's the 49ers versus the Jaguars, you up for it?"

Mackinnon hesitated, but then he shook his head. "No, I can't make it, it's Katy's birthday. She's having a party on Wednesday night for her friends, and then we're meant to be having a family dinner on Saturday."

Derek handed Mackinnon a beer. "Is she really going to be bothered if you're not there?"

Mackinnon thought for a moment. Would she? Probably not. It was more Chloe's idea of a family dinner.

"Maybe not, but I can't just blow them off," Mackinnon said. "It wouldn't be fair. Chloe has planned it all."

Derek grunted. "All right, your loss."

They took their beers back into the living room. Derek sat back on his leather recliner and Mackinnon took the sofa.

Molly padded over and curled up by Mackinnon's feet.

"I notice you don't have a bag with you tonight," Derek said.

Mackinnon frowned."Bag?"

"A supermarket bag. I thought you were on this new healthy eating regime. No more takeaways."

"Well, I didn't say *no more* takeaways," Mackinnon said. "Just *less* takeaways."

Derek raised his beer bottle and grinned. "Indian tonight then?"

Mackinnon leaned back on the sofa, closed his eyes and nodded. "Sounds good to me."

CHAPTER TWENTY

THE FOLLOWING MORNING AFTER THE early briefing, Mackinnon and Charlotte headed to Whitechapel, to speak to Adam Jonah's old boss, Bruno Moretti. If what Kofi Ayensu had told them was true, then Adam's old boss could be a strong suspect for his murder.

Bruno Moretti owned a small pizza parlour just off Whitechapel Road.

Charlotte and Mackinnon both emerged from the underground station, smothering yawns. It had been a long couple of days.

"So, what do you think of the roommate?" Charlotte asked. "Do you think he's just spinning us a line on this one, trying to shift suspicion?"

"He's got no record," Mackinnon said. "And we haven't uncovered any motive he could have for wanting to kill Adam."

Charlotte nodded. "True, but Kofi Ayensu doesn't have

many records anywhere. Nothing at the DVLA, no tax record, no national insurance contributions. He could be living under the radar for a reason."

Mackinnon nodded. "People do that for all sorts of reasons though, not just because they want to kill someone."

It was only a short walk from the station to the pizza parlour. It stood between two old red brick buildings in a glaze of bright yellow and pink and had a neon sign protruding over the entrance.

"Tasteful," Charlotte said, raising her eyebrows. "Makes it hard to miss."

"We get to go to all the great places," Mackinnon said. "Still, we shouldn't knock it until we've tried it. They might have great pizza."

Charlotte looked doubtfully through the glass window that formed the shop's frontage. "Maybe."

This early in the morning, the pizza parlour was still closed, but according to Evie Charlesworth's research, the owner had a flat above.

"Do you think this is the entrance to the flat, too?" Charlotte asked, peering in the window, shading her eyes and leaning so close to the glass that her breath left a steamy circle.

Mackinnon took a step back and looked up at the windows on the second floor, above the pizza parlour. A light was on.

"Let's just try and ring the bell," Mackinnon said. "If we don't get an answer, we can try around the back. The entrance to the flat might be at the back of the building."

He rang the bell, and they waited almost a minute.

Charlotte shook her head. "I can't hear anything. I'm not even sure if the bell is working."

Mackinnon leaned down to rattle the letterbox.

They waited.

"We'll give him another minute," Mackinnon said. "Then we'll head round the back."

A few seconds later, a bleary-eyed man appeared inside the pizza parlour, scratching his head and frowning at them through the glass.

Mackinnon took out his ID and held it up, pressing it against the glass window.

The man hesitated, his eyes flickered back to the door behind him.

Mackinnon braced himself. Perhaps one of them should have waited by the back entrance in case he made a run for it.

It was that split second, before a suspect put his or her guard up, that was the most telling. The surprise of realising that he was a police officer, made people react differently.

Almost everyone was guarded so you couldn't read too much into that. Police often delivered bad news.

But it was the desire to run that Mackinnon sensed from Bruno Moretti.

Eventually, Bruno decided better of it. His shoulders slumped, and he opened the door.

He wore an old, stained white T-shirt and a pair of boxer shorts.

"Sorry for getting you out of bed, sir. We would like a

few words with you. We are hoping you can help us with an enquiry."

Mackinnon looked down at the man's knobbly knees and hairy legs and said pointedly, "We can wait while you put your trousers on."

"Well, that is kind of you," Bruno Moretti said in an East London accent, tinged with sarcasm.

He had all the appearance of an Italian pizza parlour owner, with his dark hair and tanned skin, but by his accent, it was clear he'd lived in and around London all his life.

"What's the bloody urgency?" Moretti asked. "I've only just got out of bed. Could you not have phoned and given me a bit of warning? I would have put my trousers on at least."

He gave a nod in Charlotte's direction. "Sorry love."

"Cup of coffee might help wake you up a bit," Mackinnon said.

The man gave an annoyed look and left the door wide open for Mackinnon and Charlotte as he staggered back towards the counter, scratching his belly.

"I suppose you'll be wanting a cup of coffee, too?" Bruno asked as he switched on a large coffee machine.

Everywhere seemed to have those coffee machines these days, not only coffee shops. There was obviously a fortune in it. It wasn't a surprise they made so much when places were charging over two quid for a little cup of coffee.

"It'll heat up in a couple of minutes," Bruno said. "I'm going to go and put my trousers on."

As he left, he gave them a look over his shoulder, as if he

wasn't sure they could be trusted to be left alone in the empty pizza parlour.

At the doorway, he raised a finger. "Don't touch anything."

Mackinnon pulled out a plastic chair and sat down at a Formica covered table. He plucked idly at one of the plastic-laminated menus. It was all standard stuff: margaritas, Hawaiian and pepperoni pizzas.

Charlotte walked slowly round the room, as if she was expecting to find something.

"What do you think of him?" Charlotte asked in a low voice. "Don't you think it's weird he didn't ask us what we are here for? He didn't seem the least bit interested in asking what the enquiry was about. Maybe because he already knows."

"Maybe," Mackinnon said. "But the man has just woken up. I don't think we can read too much into it."

Charlotte pulled out a chair, inspecting it before sitting down.

Only a minute later, Bruno trundled back downstairs and strode into the kitchen area.

He didn't say anything as he stood behind the counter. He pressed a few buttons on the huge coffee machine, and the contraption began to make an awful wheezing noise.

He waited until the machine stopped gurgling, and then carried three little cups of espresso over to the Formica table. Placing one in front of Mackinnon and one beside Charlotte, he sat down opposite them.

He took a sip of his coffee.

"Ah, that's better," he said. "These late nights and early

mornings. It gets harder as you get older. I can't do the late nights like I used to."

He blinked as if the coffee was slowly clearing his head. "What's this all about then?"

"It's about an old employee of yours."

Bruno grunted. "Well, I've had a few of those. Maybe you could narrow it down for me and tell me which one?"

"Adam Jonah," Mackinnon said.

"Adam?" The man nodded. "Well, I'm not likely to forget him. What has he done this time?"

Charlotte and Mackinnon didn't answer.

Charlotte leaned forward and took a sip of her coffee. She paused as though she was slowly savouring the taste, then she said, "We've heard you had an argument with him last week."

Bruno snorted. "I did more than had an argument. I sacked his lazy arse."

"Why was that?" Charlotte asked.

Bruno waved a hand. "Oh, I don't want to go into it all again. It just winds me up. It's no good for my blood pressure."

His face *was* looking a little pink.

"Well, we would like you to talk about it," Charlotte said.

Bruno frowned. "Why? Why are you interested? Look, if it's about tax and all that stuff…" Bruno held up his hands. "I just took him on for a trial. If he passed the trial, I was going to set it up properly. All above board and sign him on the books."

"It's not about your books," Mackinnon said. "Adam Jonah has been murdered."

Charlotte and Mackinnon both studied Bruno Moretti's face. The man seemed to go pale beneath his tanned skin.

Bruno licked his lips. "Adam? Are you sure?"

Mackinnon inclined his head. "We're sure. Now we'd like to know about this argument you had with him."

Bruno ran a hand through his thinning hair, pushed his coffee cup away and shook his head.

"You think his murder has something to do with me. Well, it hasn't. Look, I admit that we had an argument. A major bust up, but the little bastard was stealing from me. I had to sack him, didn't I?"

Bruno looked at Charlotte, appealing for her agreement.

Charlotte said nothing.

"I've done nothing wrong! All I'm doing is trying to earn an honest living, and I just can't get the staff. He was the last straw. I was going to come to the police and report him. But I didn't as I'm too bloody soft."

Charlotte and Mackinnon said nothing, waiting for Bruno to continue. He was clearly feeling uncomfortable and uncomfortable people tended to babble, revealing more than they intended to.

"I know what you're thinking. I can see it in the way you're looking at me. All right, I was mad at him. He stole from me and that pissed me off. But I wouldn't have killed him over it. It was only two hundred nicker. Hardly worth killing someone over."

"Look, I didn't even report it to you lot. I just let him off. To tell you the truth, I felt sorry for him."

"Sorry for him? Why?" Mackinnon asked.

"Because he fed me a sob story. He told me he needed the money and that he was planning on hiring a solicitor.

"He wanted to see his son, and his nasty ex was stopping him. In fact…" Bruno leaned forward over the Formica table top. "You probably wanna have a chat with her. From what Adam said, she was a right nasty piece of work."

"Adam's ex. Ex what? Ex-wife? Ex-Girlfriend?"

Bruno paused and frowned. "Well, I don't think he ever told me that. I don't know if they married. But if they did, she didn't take his name."

Bruno pulled his coffee cup towards him, studying the brown dregs in the bottom of the cup.

"No, I don't think they were married," Bruno said, looking up. "Nah, pretty sure they weren't. Apparently, she's gone and got married to this old, rich plastic surgeon. They've got a massive house and live near Kensington, I think. I don't know the exact address. But she's rolling in it now. And she doesn't want anything to do with Adam anymore."

Bruno hesitated, realising what he'd said.

"I suppose she's got her wish now, hasn't she?"

CHAPTER TWENTY-ONE

AFTER CALLING INTO WOOD STREET Station and speaking to Tyler, giving him the name of Adam Jonah's ex-partner, it hadn't been long before the team had tracked down the woman's address.

After receiving the information, Mackinnon and Charlotte headed off towards Kensington High Street on the tube. Their Oyster cards were seeing plenty of action today.

Adam Jonah's ex-partner was a woman called Joy Barter. Bruno Moretti said the name had stuck in his mind because Adam went on so much about the fact her name was Joy when she'd brought Adam anything but.

But Joy Barter had obviously moved up in the world after dating Adam.

Just off Kensington High Street, Mackinnon and Charlotte stood at the bottom of a set of polished marble steps that led up to a huge town house.

"Clearly, plastic surgery pays well," Charlotte said as they climbed the steps.

She rang the ornate bell on the huge green door.

A moment later, the door was opened by a young woman with shoulder-length fair hair.

She had a little boy, aged two or three, sitting on her hip.

"Joy Barter?" Mackinnon asked.

Mackinnon and Charlotte held up their IDs.

"No, I'm the nanny, Lucy Sampson. Mrs. Barter is inside."

"We'd like a word with Mrs. Barter, please."

The nanny nodded and stood back, opening the door wider, so they could come in.

The little boy stared up at them with big chocolate brown eyes.

Charlotte gave him a smile, and the boy shyly turned his head into the nanny's neck.

"Who is it, Lucy?"

They heard a sharp woman's voice coming from another room down the hallway.

The nanny shot them an embarrassed look.

"If you don't mind waiting, I'll just tell Mrs. Barter you're here," she said.

Heaving the boy onto her other hip, she walked swiftly along the corridor.

Mackinnon looked up and took in the grand surroundings. They stood on a polished marble floor, and a huge chandelier hung above them.

"Must be a hell of a place to dust," Mackinnon muttered.

He couldn't even imagine what a house of this size, in this location, would cost.

They heard Mrs. Barter telling the nanny, in a dismissive tone, to go and make some tea. Then they heard footsteps, and a moment later Joy Barter walked towards them with her hand outstretched.

She was certainly a striking woman. She was at least five-foot ten and towered over Charlotte.

"I'm Mrs. Barter," she said as she shook their hands. "How can I help you?"

They needed to approach this carefully. Joy Barter may have ended her relationship with Adam Jonah, but he was still her son's father. The news of his death would come as a shock.

"Perhaps we could sit down," Mackinnon said.

The smile slipped from Joy's face. "Something has happened, hasn't it? An accident? Is it my husband?"

In a daze, she led them along the hallway, and then into a huge room with floor to ceiling windows looking out over the garden.

She sat down and put her hands on her knees. Her hands were shaking.

"What is keeping that girl?" she said, in an irritated tone.

Joy Barter raised a perfectly manicured hand and began to chew on a red fingernail. She frowned when she realised what she was doing and clasped both hands in her lap.

"Well, what is it?" she demanded. "What has happened?"

"I'm afraid we've got some bad news," Mackinnon said. "Adam Jonah is dead."

For a fraction of a second, there was a flicker of what looked like relief on Joy Barter's face, which was quickly followed by a heavy frown.

"And what's that got to do with me?"

"We were led to believe you had been in a relationship with Adam Jonah."

Joy Barter rolled her eyes. "A long time ago. I'm married now."

Charlotte was surprised at Joy Barter's reaction. For most people, hearing about the death of even a casual acquaintance would elicit a more emotional response than that.

They all looked up as the nanny entered with the tea. She set down the tray on a small coffee table.

"Shall I pour?" she asked, looking at Joy Barter.

Joy waved a hand at the girl. "Yes. This is Lucy Sampson," she said to Mackinnon and Charlotte. "She's our nanny. She's been with us for six months. She can tell you I've not seen Adam in all that time."

The little boy was still clinging to the nanny's leg, staring at Charlotte and Mackinnon with big round eyes.

"And who is this little chap?" Charlotte asked, leaning towards the little boy. "What's your name?"

"Thomas," Joy Barter said.

Charlotte waited a moment, but there was no more information forthcoming. "Is he Adam's little boy?" she asked.

Joy Barter's face screwed up. She looked as if she'd

sucked a lemon. "I suppose you could say that. But he hasn't been involved in Thomas's upbringing at all."

"By choice?" Mackinnon asked.

"If you knew Adam," Joy said. "You'd know he'd be a terrible influence on a young boy. He's a deadbeat. A waste of space. He's no kind of role model for my son."

Mackinnon couldn't help noticing she was referring to Adam in the present tense, as if she still felt she had to defend her son from him.

"We have to tell you that Adam was murdered," Charlotte said.

Joy Barter blinked took a deep breath and kept her eyes on the floor as she leaned forward to pick up her tea.

Her cup rattled against the saucer. "Murdered?"

She took a sip of her tea and put it down, putting a hand to her mouth to smother a sob. "Even when he's dead, Adam's still trying to ruin my life," she said.

Mackinnon and Charlotte exchanged glances. That was a very odd thing to say.

Joy Barter ran her hands across her skirt and seemed to gather herself. "Do you know who did it?"

"Not yet," Mackinnon said. "But we are investigating a number of good leads."

She nodded. "I don't have any information. If that's what you've come here for, you're out of luck.

"I have no idea who killed him, but he mixed in some dodgy circles, and he was always managing to piss people off."

The little boy looked up at his mother and said, "Bad word."

Joy Barter narrowed her eyes. "Take him to the play-room, Lucy." She snapped at the nanny, who'd been hovering by the door.

"Did Adam ever mention a Mr. X to you?" Charlotte asked.

Joy wrinkled her nose. "Mr. X?"

"We think he was a spirit guide Adam was using."

"No, I've never heard of Mr. X. What a ridiculous name. It sounds like a character in a comic!"

Mackinnon had to agree with her there. He still wasn't convinced that Kofi had been telling them the truth.

She shook her head. "Is that who you think killed Adam? You don't have much to go on, do you? I hope this isn't one of your good leads."

Joy Barter leaned back in her armchair and pinched the bridge of her nose between her thumb and forefinger.

"I think I'm getting one of my migraines," she said. "I can't believe this is happening."

Charlotte and Mackinnon managed to ask a few more questions before leaving Joy Barter with her migraine.

As they trudged down the marble steps and headed out towards Kensington High Street, Charlotte turned to Mackinnon.

"Have you ever met anyone as cold or calculating as that? That little boy's dad is dead, and she just snaps at the nanny telling her to take him to the playroom.

"He'll never know his dad. He'll never know that his dad was fighting to see him. I mean, he'll have all this…" Charlotte gestured behind them at the row of terraced townhouses.

"I'm sure the money is very nice, but how's that going to make up for never knowing his real dad."

Mackinnon shrugged. "I feel sorry for the nanny. Imagine having to work for that woman."

Charlotte zipped up her coat. "Do you think she was involved in Adam's death?"

"Well, it's very unlikely Joy Barter would have had the strength to kill him on her own," Mackinnon said. "But that doesn't mean she wasn't involved."

CHAPTER TWENTY-TWO

ALFIE HAD CREPT BACK INTO the flat at two o'clock in the morning.

He had waited outside, shivering in the cold, until he saw all the lights had been switched off, and he was sure his aunt and uncle would be asleep.

He'd let himself in as quietly as possible, tiptoeing to his room. He stripped off his rain-sodden clothes and tumbled into bed.

He pulled the duvet cover over his head, so he'd be able to set the alarm on his phone. He didn't want the light from the screen to wake anyone up, but it was essential he set the alarm. He needed to make sure he was up first in the morning and out of here.

He selected the vibration alert. That would have less chance of waking Aunt Erika or Uncle Remi in the morning.

Alfie didn't know if they were just threatening to take him to Mr. X to scare him. He thought they might have said it to try and make Alfie behave himself. Maybe they had no intention of taking him to Mr. X. But Alfie didn't want to take the chance.

He had lain in bed staring up at the ceiling for a long time. Every creak and rattle in the flat had sent his heart pounding. He heard his uncle's rumbling snores, coming from the room next door.

Alfie had bitten his lip and tried to imagine Mickey playing at the beach at Southend. He pictured him, running away from the waves on the shore, and having an ice-cream. Alfie smiled. It would be chocolate. It was his favourite.

Alfie had still been thinking of his little brother when he drifted off to sleep.

It felt like he'd only closed his eyes for a few seconds, when the buzz of the alarm woke him. He frantically searched the bed for his phone, so he could turn off the alarm before it woke anyone else.

He had pressed the reset button and then sat rigidly in bed, waiting to hear footsteps or telltale signs that his aunt or uncle had woken up.

But there was nothing.

He couldn't hear his uncle's snores, though. That probably meant he was only sleeping lightly. Alfie was desperate for the bathroom, but he couldn't risk it. He would just have to wait.

Alfie dressed as quickly as he could, making as little noise as possible, and left the house before six a.m.

It was still dark, and Alfie had three hours to kill before school started and nowhere to go.

But, first things first.

He jogged to Rickman's bakery on the corner of Hart Street. They had a public toilet, and Alfie was busting.

The woman behind the counter eyed him warily as he came in.

"You're a bit early for school, aren't you love?"

She watched as Alfie selected a can of coke from the chilled cabinet.

"You want anything to eat with that, love?" the woman said, tapping in Alfie's order on the till.

"Um…" Alfie looked up at the sign by the till, advertising 'bacon sandwiches' in swirly writing. His mouth watered, and he stared down at the coins in the palm of his hand. He was five pence short.

"No," he said. "I haven't got enough."

"Give us a look," the woman peered at the money in Alfie's hand. Then she looked up and pursed her lips.

She gave a big theatrical sigh, then said, "Go on, then. Just this once. I'll let you owe me the five. You want a bacon sarnie, right?"

Alfie nodded and poured all of his coins into the woman's hand.

"Can I use your toilet?" he asked.

"Of course you can, love. It's just round the back."

Alfie walked behind the counter and rushed into the toilet at the back. He couldn't wait to get his teeth into the bacon sandwich. He'd been feeling too anxious to eat for the past few days, but now he was starving.

After using the toilet, Alfie wolfed down his bacon sandwich and drank his Coke in tiny sips, dragging out his time in the warm cafe. But eventually the cafe started to fill up, and Alfie felt bad about taking up a table when the woman had been so nice to him.

So he had left, and to kill time, he'd walked around the Towers Estate three times, meandering in and out of the alleyways. He zipped his jacket all the way up to his chin and looked up at the grey clouds. At least the rain had stopped.

Although the morning dragged, his day at school went far too quickly, and Alfie was fast running out of time to decide what to do.

By lunchtime, he was sure he should go to the nearest police station and tell them what had happened, but an hour later, he changed his mind again.

What if they didn't believe him? What if the police phoned his aunt and uncle, and they punished him for telling tales.

Even if the police did believe him, what could they do?

They'd still have to tell his aunt and uncle. No matter how many times Alfie tried to work it out in his head, he couldn't see a way out of this mess.

Alfie's head ached and his throat was sore. He was probably getting a cold, he thought, because he'd gotten soaked to the skin last night. His grandmother had always told him not to stay out in the rain.

By three p.m., Alfie knew he had to go and speak to his grandmother.

She was the only one that would be able to help him. He didn't have enough money for the train, but he'd borrowed enough money from his friend Stuart to make the phone call.

He didn't have any credit left on his mobile phone, and the stupid pay-as-you-go phone only allowed top ups in ten pound increments. So after school, Alfie had walked to the parade of shops, near where Mr. Xander had caught Francis smoking, and searched for a functional phone box.

Alfie was out of luck. Both phone booths were unusable. They had been vandalised, and there was a definite whiff of urine around them. But worse than that, neither phone box took coins. Only cards.

It was a sign. Alfie chewed on a nail. It was a sign that he shouldn't call his grandmother.

Alfie wandered around the streets for another hour, not wanting to go back to his uncle and aunt's flat, but not having anywhere else to go.

He briefly considered not going back at all, but last night's freezing rainy weather had shown him that wasn't the best option.

He'd have to go back to the flat and speak to Aunt Erika. He had to convince her that he wasn't possessed, that he was trying to be good.

Maybe he could ask her if he could have some money for a trip to go and see his grandmother.

Alfie made his way back to the flat. He still had another couple of hours before Uncle Remi was due home. That meant he had a chance. He'd just have to be persuasive.

Alfie slipped his key in the lock and turned it quietly. He winced when the front door creaked as it opened.

Alfie froze as he heard his aunt talking inside the flat. His heart pounded. Had Uncle Remi come home early?

Were they going to punish him now? Were they waiting for Alfie to come home so they could take him to Mr. X?

Alfie waited there in the doorway. The cold draught from the landing whistled between his legs as he listened.

It was only his aunt's voice he could hear. She was laughing, and she seemed happy.

Alfie took a step inside, but he kept his hand on the door, still not willing to let it shut behind him and block his exit.

Then he heard his aunt speak again.

"I know Mother," she said.

Alfie felt a little jolt of hope when he realised she must be talking to his grandmother.

Was she here?

Alfie shut the door quietly behind him and moved forward to hear more of the conversation.

"Oh, don't you worry. We've got him in check. He's a bad one, but we won't let it beat us," Aunt Erika said.

Alfie froze.

She was talking about him.

"Yes, I know he was too much work for you," she was saying. "You don't have the energy, I know that. It's not your fault. You haven't let anyone down. The boy has got some evil in him."

Alfie slipped past the open doorway to the living room and went straight into his bedroom and closed the door.

He didn't want to hear any more.

CHAPTER TWENTY-THREE

EVERYTHING THAT COULD POSSIBLY GO wrong on Wednesday night did.

Despite being on the early shift, Mackinnon hadn't managed to leave the station until six-thirty, and even then he would have preferred to stay, but he'd promised to get back for Katy's birthday party.

He'd taken the train back to Oxford, which was a mistake. There'd been a tree across a line somewhere which had led to his train being stationary for half an hour.

He sat on the train, checking the time on his phone every few minutes. It was such a waste. He could have been working.

The train had stopped in an area with absolutely no mobile phone reception. All around him in the carriage, people where fruitlessly trying to get a signal. One man was even holding his phone above his head and waving it around.

It was funny how over the past few years, almost everyone had become addicted to using their phones. Sometimes at the expense of interacting with friends you were with at the time. He'd noticed friends break away, during a pause in conversation, to check on their phones.

It seemed people found it impossible to do without them for even a few minutes.

He'd taken a taxi from Oxford. He wasn't about to wait for the bus. He was late already.

It was eight p.m. before Mackinnon finally arrived at Chloe's house on Woodstock Road.

The house was warm and smelt of candyfloss.

He could hear the sound of giggling girls in the front room. Obviously Katy's party was in full swing. He didn't want to intrude so he opened the door just enough to lean inside and wish her happy birthday.

Mackinnon couldn't put his finger on it at first, but there was something that felt strange, something odd about the setup.

Katy's friends, all five of them, were crammed onto a three-seater sofa while Katy sat alone on the two-seater. Wrapping paper was crumpled around her ankles where she'd obviously opened her presents.

"Happy birthday, sweetheart," he said.

Katy looked up, gave a little smile, then said, "Thanks Jack."

He ducked out again, not wanting to intrude, and made his way to the kitchen where he got the shock of his life.

Chloe was standing at the kitchen counter, finishing off some toffee apples and adding sprinkles.

She wore a short black dress and a sparkly green wig with bright green tights to match. Her outfit was topped off with a pointed witch's hat.

"Nice costume," he said. "You've got into the party spirit."

She shot him a look. A look that told him she wasn't happy.

"I tried to get back as quickly as I could."

"Mmmhmm," Chloe said with a flick of her green hair. "You'll find *your* outfit upstairs."

Mackinnon's mouth dropped open. "My outfit? Seriously?"

Chloe gave him a self-satisfied smile. "Yes."

Mackinnon headed upstairs to their bedroom, and on the bed on top of the duvet, he found a neatly folded black cape and a pair of plastic fangs.

He flung the cape around his shoulders, avoiding the mirror as he walked out of the bedroom. He didn't want to see himself looking like an idiot. He imagined DC Webb would love to get a photo of him in this getup and use it for blackmail.

He decided not to put the fangs in yet. He shoved them in his pocket and headed back downstairs.

He picked up a sausage roll as he walked back into the kitchen. "Is the party going well?" Mackinnon asked. "Are they having a good time?"

Chloe shrugged. "I think so. I can't really tell with Katy sometimes. She seems a little quiet."

"Where's Sarah?" Mackinnon asked before demolishing the sausage roll.

Chloe visibly tensed. "She hasn't come home yet, and she *promised* to be here."

Mackinnon caught the subtext. She promised to be here in time for the party just as he had.

"I'm gonna go and take these in." She lifted the plateful of toffee apples. "Don't eat all of those," she said, nodding at the plate of sausage rolls Mackinnon was steadily working his way through.

Mackinnon gave her a hurt *'as if I would'* look.

As soon as she left the kitchen, Mackinnon picked up another sausage roll and then smothered a yawn.

He wondered what time Chloe had arranged for the other girls to go home. Surely it wouldn't be too late. They were only kids.

Mackinnon really needed to get an early night because he had to be up at stupid o'clock tomorrow to get into London for his early shift.

He turned as Chloe walked back into the kitchen, still carrying the plate of toffee apples.

"I thought you were taking them in to the girls," he said.

Chloe looked very pale.

She put the plate down and leaned over the kitchen sink, gripping the edge so tightly her knuckles turned white.

"What's wrong?"

She shook her head. "I overheard them. They are supposed to be her friends, but they are sitting in there making bitchy comments about Katy's hair. All of them. They're ganging up on her."

"Are you sure?" Mackinnon walked over to Chloe's side. "Maybe it's just good-natured teasing."

"There was nothing good-natured about it." Chloe turned to face him. "They are bullying her."

Mackinnon paused and took a breath. "Well, why don't we go in there? They won't do it in front of us, will they?"

Chloe clenched her fists. "I don't think I can, Jack. I'm so angry. I won't be able to not say anything."

"Okay," Mackinnon said, picking up the plate of toffee apples. "I'll take them in."

Chloe turned and leaned back against the kitchen counter. "Thanks."

Before Mackinnon could leave the kitchen, Katy entered and stared at the toffee apples.

"What are those for? I can't believe it. I'm not a child! No wonder they're all laughing at me."

Katy's face was pink, and her eyes were shiny with unshed tears.

"You used to love toffee apples," Chloe said.

"Yeah," Katy said. "When I was a *kid*."

"Don't be ridiculous. Toffee apples are not just for children," Chloe said.

She picked one up and took a large bite, smearing her lips with the caramel coating, which hadn't quite set.

"And what are you wearing?" Katy said looking at her, and then turning her eyes on Mackinnon. "Even you, Jack? You look stupid."

"Hang on a minute, young lady," Chloe said. "This is what you wanted. You asked for a fancy dress party. I spent ages trying to get these costumes..." Chloe trailed off and seemed to notice that Katy wasn't wearing her costume. "We got you a skeleton outfit. Why have you taken it off?"

Katy turned around. "You don't understand," she said.

She stalked out of the kitchen and back into the sitting room.

Mackinnon took his cape off. "I guess it's not a fancy dress party any more then."

Chloe took off the witch's hat, pulled off the green wig and fluffed up her fair hair.

"I don't know what's got into her. She was so excited about this party. Even last night she was full of beans. We carved pumpkins after school." Chloe flung the witch's hat on the counter. "She used to love all this stuff."

"I guess she's growing up," Mackinnon said and stabbed at a sausage roll with a fork.

Chloe pulled the tray of sausage rolls away from him.

"It's not that," she said. "It's those little girls in there. Teasing her. They're nothing but a bunch of bullies. She was really excited about this party before they arrived."

Mackinnon was regretting eating so many sausage rolls. He rubbed his chest as a wave of heartburn hit him full force. He put his hands in his pockets looking for Rennies.

"She just wants her friends to think she's a grown up," Mackinnon said. "I know it's not very nice when you've gone to all this trouble and done all this work."

Chloe shook her head. "It's not that, I don't mind doing it. I just don't understand how she could have changed her mind so quickly."

Chloe and Mackinnon stayed in the kitchen until the first of the parents showed up to collect their daughters.

Once all the teenagers had gone, Chloe seemed to relax a little.

For the rest of the evening, Katy was very quiet.

Mackinnon sat on the sofa and could barely keep his eyes open, as Chloe probed Katy, asking questions and trying to find out what the girls had said to make her change her mind about the fancy dress party.

But Katy wasn't very talkative.

When Chloe went out to make coffee, Mackinnon felt the sofa dip beside him. He opened one eye and saw Katy sitting on the edge of the sofa next to him.

"Are you all right, sweetheart? Did you have a nice time tonight?"

"Not really," Katy said.

Mackinnon opened both eyes. He knew he should be asking questions, but he didn't know the right ones to ask.

As she sat there looking miserable, Mackinnon felt a tenderness for the poor kid. He would have done just about anything to make her birthday happier.

Was Katy having a bad time at school? Were the girls that she invited to her birthday party really ganging up on her?

Popularity was all so important at that age. He wanted to say something reassuring or helpful, but he was crap at this sort of thing.

"Well, I'm looking forward to Saturday. Where do you fancy going? My treat."

Katy shrugged.

"Come on. There must be somewhere you want to go."

"Byron's?" Katy raised her head. "The burgers are nice there and they do a cookie flavour milkshake"

"Okay. Byron's it is."

Katy curled her legs up on the sofa. "I'm sorry for what I said earlier. You know, about your vampire costume."

"That's all right. I did look a bit stupid. You know that if there is something bothering you, you can talk to me or your mum."

Katy shrugged and reached for the TV remote. "I know," she said. "But there isn't anything. I'm fine."

She switched on the television, flicking through the channels, and Mackinnon guessed the conversation was over.

CHAPTER TWENTY-FOUR

WHEN MACKINNON GOT TO WOOD Street the following morning, he was shattered. The commute from Oxford to London in the early hours had been quiet, but he had found it very difficult to get out of bed that morning.

He sat in the briefing room next to Charlotte and waited for Tyler to make a start.

Mackinnon was already on his third coffee of the day. He raised his cup and breathed in the aroma before taking a sip, but so far the caffeine wasn't having its usual effect.

He was going to need a pot of coffee at this rate.

Tyler started off the briefing, and everyone gave updates in turn.

They had no new leads from Francis Eze's phone or computer.

Rosialie Estes, the family liaison officer, had spoken to Francis's parents, Mr. and Mrs. Eze, and asked them whether they had heard Francis mention a Mr. X.

Francis's father said he'd never heard the name, but Francis's mother said she'd heard Francis mention it once or twice. She didn't think he was a real person. When she heard Francis mention Mr. X, she had assumed he was referring to a character in a film or a TV show.

Rosialie had also shown Mr. and Mrs. Eze a photograph of Adam Jonah, to see if they recognised him. Unfortunately, they didn't.

Tyler wasn't happy.

"There has to be a link between them," he said. "If we find that, we'll be able to make some progress."

The rest of the team had been methodically raking through financial and phone records, looking for any links between the two victims, but so far, they'd found nothing.

But Evie Charlesworth had uncovered something interesting.

When Tyler nodded for her to speak up, she told the team she'd been trawling through Joy Barter's financial records and had discovered the woman had made a cash withdrawal for five thousand pounds last week.

Now that was interesting. Mackinnon took a sip of his coffee and watched Tyler's reaction.

"We need to find out what that money was for," Tyler said. He looked to Mackinnon and Charlotte. "Go back and pay Joy Barter a visit this morning. Find out what that money was for."

Mackinnon nodded. A withdrawal like that was unusual. People didn't tend to deal much in cash these days, especially not someone married to a mega-rich plastic surgeon who lived in Kensington. Mackinnon was willing to bet she had a few platinum cards stashed in her purse.

So what would a woman like Joy Barter have needed that five thousand pounds for?

Tyler moved on, assigning new tasks, and DCI Brookbank joined them for the last ten minutes of the meeting.

He said nothing but kept his deep-set, hooded eyes on them all.

After Brookbank arrived in the briefing room, Tyler continually tugged at his shirt, as if his tie was too tight around his neck. Mackinnon felt for him. This was a tough case, and Tyler had never been an officer who enjoyed responsibility. Over the past few months, more and more tasks had been piled onto Tyler's shoulders. Mackinnon didn't envy him his detective inspector's role.

Mackinnon would be glad to go and speak to Joy Barter again. The last thing he wanted was to sit at a desk trawling through paperwork. He was so tired he thought he'd probably miss something, and they couldn't afford to do that in an investigation like this.

Charlotte and Mackinnon decided to go by tube again. It was so much easier to take public transport than to try and drive in central London, and actually in most cases, it was quicker.

When they arrived at the Kensington town house, the door was answered by the nanny as before. This time there was no little boy on her hip.

"Lucy, isn't it?" Mackinnon asked, showing his ID again.

"Yes, that's right, Lucy Sampson," she said.

"Where's Thomas today?" Charlotte asked.

"Having a nap. He had a bad night."

"Did you ever meet Thomas's father?" Mackinnon asked as Lucy stepped back to let them into the house.

Lucy looked over her shoulder as though she was scared Joy Barter might overhear their conversation.

She shook her head. "No."

"Did Mrs. Barter tell you Thomas's father has been killed?"

Lucy nodded. "She didn't exactly tell me. I overheard some of your conversation."

Mackinnon handed her a card.

"If there's anything you think of that might help us find out what happened to Thomas's father, you can call me on that number," Mackinnon said and nodded at the card in her hand.

"Like what?" Lucy Sampson's eyes darted between Mackinnon and Charlotte. "I don't know anything, I'm just the nanny."

They heard Joy Barter's heels clacking on the marble floor before she appeared in the hallway.

She was wearing some kind of power suit with heavy shoulder pads that Mackinnon thought had gone out in the eighties. Her dark hair was slicked back today, showing off her cheekbones. Her lips were painted a deep red.

Joy Barter held one carefully manicured hand to the side of her face when she saw Charlotte and Mackinnon.

"Oh, it's you," she said. "Back again so soon?"

"Yes," Mackinnon nodded. "We've got a few more questions for you, if you don't mind?"

"I suppose I don't have much of a choice," Joy Barter

said, gesturing for them to walk ahead of her and into the sitting room.

"Would you like some tea or coffee?"

They shook their heads and Joy Barter dismissed Lucy Sampson with a nod.

The nanny left, closing the door behind her.

"So," Joy Barter said, resting her hands in her lap. "What is it I can do for you this time?"

"I wondered if you had any more thoughts on who may have wanted to hurt Adam," Mackinnon said.

"I already told you everything I know. I wasn't a part of Adam's life anymore. I really can't be of any help to you," Joy Barter said. "And I must tell you that I've spoken to my husband, and he isn't happy with you harassing me like this. If you insist on asking more questions, I'll have to have my lawyer with me."

Mackinnon raised an eyebrow. "We're not harassing you. We're simply asking a few questions about your ex-partner. Your son's father."

Joy straightened in her chair. "It feels like harassment to me. I don't want anything to do with this, and I don't want my little boy picking up on this negativity."

Negativity? That wasn't how Mackinnon would have described it.

Joy Barter sat forward in her chair. "Are we done?" she asked.

"Not quite," Mackinnon said. "I have one more question."

Joy Barter sighed. "Well, if you could hurry up and ask your last question, I do have places to be today."

"You made a withdrawal of five thousand pounds in cash last week."

Mackinnon let his words sink in as Joy Barter's eyes grew wide and round. "You've been looking at my bank account?"

Her shock soon turned to anger. "How dare you? I suppose you love snooping around in other people's affairs. I bet you get off on it."

Mackinnon ignored her comment. "What was the money for?"

"It's none of your damn business, that's what it was for."

"If you've nothing to hide, I can't see why you can't tell us why you needed that amount of money in cash," Mackinnon said.

Joy Barter bit down on her lower lip, and her gaze flitted up to the window. For a few seconds, she said nothing then she turned back and faced Charlotte.

"Look, it wasn't anything that would interest you. Nothing to do with Adam at all. It was for a new handbag. I'd wanted it for ages and decided to treat myself."

"Why use cash?" Charlotte asked. "I'm sure you've got lots of charge cards."

Joy scowled. "My husband doesn't really understand anything to do with fashion. He's careful with money, and he doesn't like me buying expensive bags and shoes. If I want something, I take the cash from our bank account, and he doesn't see what the money was for. He assumes it's for household bills."

Household bills? Who had household bills for that amount?

Joy shrugged. "There's nothing illegal about it. No one gets hurt, and it's not as if he can't afford it."

"Do you mind showing us this new bag?" Mackinnon asked.

Joy's head shot up. "You want to see the bag... Why?"

"Humour me," Mackinnon said.

Joy Barter hesitated, then she shrugged and got up out of her chair.

"Very well," she said. "I'll be back in a moment."

As soon as Joy Barter left the room, the nanny, Lucy Sampson, appeared at the doorway. The little boy had woken from his nap and was clamped to her leg, peering at them with sleepy eyes. Lucy looked nervous and hesitant, and Mackinnon guessed she wanted to tell them something.

Charlotte waved at the little boy, and after a moment's hesitation, he overcame his shyness and walked towards her on unsteady legs.

He held out a little toy train, and Charlotte took it. To the little boy's delight, she made a noise like a steam engine as she pushed it along the ground. Funny how we all still recognised the sound, Mackinnon thought, even though modern trains sounded nothing like that.

Mackinnon turned his attention to Lucy. "Do you like working here?"

Lucy shrugged and reached down to stroke the little boy's hair. "He's a lovely little boy," she said, not really answering the question.

"Where are you from?"

"Originally, I'm from Nottingham, but I went to Bath to

train as a Norland Nanny. I left six months ago. This is my first job."

Mackinnon pitied her. He imagined Joy Barter was not the ideal boss for a first job. For any job come to that.

When Joy Barter arrived back in the room, Lucy fell silent. Joy strode towards Mackinnon and Charlotte. Dangling from her fingertips was a dark green patterned leather bag.

"Here you go. This is the bag. Satisfied?"

"I don't suppose you still have the receipt?" Mackinnon asked.

Joy pursed her lips. "No." She reached up to smooth back her hair. "I don't have it. I don't keep receipts."

"May I?" Charlotte asked, reaching out to take the bag. "It's a lovely handbag," she said. "It's very well made."

Joy nodded. "Yes, it is. It's one of my favourites."

After Charlotte had examined the bag, they thanked Joy Barter for her time and stood up. Lucy Sampson showed them to the door. Mackinnon still had the definite impression Lucy wanted to tell them something.

He hesitated, once Joy Barter was out of earshot, giving her the opportunity, but Lucy still didn't say anything.

As they walked down the marble steps to the street, Mackinnon turned again and said, "Remember if there's anything you want to tell us, you've got my number."

Lucy looked behind her guiltily, then nodded.

They began to walk back towards High Street Kensington and Mackinnon said, "That nanny knows something."

Charlotte frowned. "You're right. I feel sorry for her. Having to work for that woman must be an awful job.

"There's definitely something going on," Charlotte continued. "There is no way Joy Barter bought that bag a week ago."

Mackinnon turned. "No? How do you know that?"

"Did you see the handles?"

"The handles? Yes, but I didn't notice anything special about them."

"It's the colour," Charlotte said. "They were a deep tan colour. The handles on a normal Louis Vuitton bag, when they are brand-new, are very, very pale.

"The handles on that bag had been darkened with use. There is no way she bought that bag a week ago." Charlotte said.

"So, she's lying to us," Mackinnon said. "The question is, why? What is she trying to hide?"

CHAPTER TWENTY-FIVE

THEY WERE JUST METRES AWAY from the High Street Kensington Underground Station, when Charlotte's mobile rang.

She stopped, ducking into a doorway to answer it.

"It's Tyler," she said, before picking up.

Mackinnon listened to her one-sided conversation as people wandered past them. He peered into the window of a health food shop called Whole Foods, examining the brown lentils and piles of turnips they had in the window. He supposed it might do him some good to start buying organic food and cooking from scratch during the week. It didn't look very appetising, though.

When Charlotte had finished the call, she shoved her phone in her pocket and joined Mackinnon at the shop window.

"Apparently, DC Webb's stumbled onto a lead from the financial trail," she said. "He hasn't had time to go and speak to the Oracle yet, so Tyler wants me to go, now."

"And me?" Mackinnon asked.

"No, apparently he needs you to go back to the station and help Collins."

Mackinnon made a face. "Paperwork?"

"I'm afraid so," Charlotte said.

Inside the underground station, they went their separate ways.

Charlotte rapped on the door to number thirty-six, and as before, the door was opened by the Oracle's son, Kwame Okoro.

Charlotte could hear the murmur of multiple voices coming from inside.

She peered over Kwame's shoulder. "I wondered if I could talk to your father again?"

Kwame stood to one side. "Come in. He's in the middle of a ceremony at the moment. Do you mind waiting until he's finished? It shouldn't take long."

"Of course," Charlotte said.

"Would you like a cup of coffee?" Kwame offered.

She nodded and followed Kwame to the kitchen. The sound of murmuring voices grew stronger, and the heavy scent of burning incense made Charlotte's eyes water.

It was much warmer inside the kitchen. Charlotte shrugged off her jacket.

She leaned back on the kitchen counter and watched as Kwame made the coffee.

"More questions for my father?" Kwame said. "Is it about the same case?"

Charlotte nodded. "Yes, I'm hoping he can answer a question for me. Do you know much about the religion yourself?" Charlotte asked, although she thought she already knew the answer to that question. He had openly shown his disdain for his father's religion the last time Charlotte had been here.

Kwame handed her a coffee and a smile teased at the corner of his mouth.

"You mean Voodoo," he said. "Not really. It's not my cup of tea."

He took a sip of his coffee and Charlotte raised her own cup, breathing in the warm scent before taking a sip and burning her tongue.

"Have you heard of a Mr. X?" she asked.

Kwame frowned and set down his coffee cup on the counter. "No. Should I have?"

"I wondered if it was something to do with the religion, maybe something to do with a ritual. I tried googling it, but I've not had much luck."

Kwame shrugged. "I can't say I've heard of anything like that related to Voodoo. It sounds more like the name of a comic superhero to me."

Charlotte smiled. "Yes, it does sound a little far-fetched."

"Sorry, I can't be more help."

Charlotte shrugged. It was worth a try. Maybe she'd have better luck with the Oracle.

"Does your dad always hold ceremonies in your house?" Charlotte asked.

Kwame shook his head. "No, only now and again. Big ceremonies are held in the community centre, but small gatherings, like this, purification rituals or rituals for luck, are all held here."

Charlotte nodded, she could hear chanting voices more distinctly now. They almost sounded angry. A chill ran along her spine.

The chanting of voices suddenly got louder as the door across the hallway opened and a woman, almost as wide as she was tall and wearing a bright red turban and a heavy necklace made out of conch shells, appeared.

She beamed at them both and then rummaged in an oversized patchwork bag. She pulled out a set of car keys and held them out for Kwame.

"Be a sweet boy and bring my car around, will you? I had to park on Queen Street."

Kwame did what he was told. Charlotte had the impression this woman was used to people doing what she asked.

After Kwame left the kitchen, the woman groaned and pulled out a stool from under the breakfast bar.

"I need to rest my feet," she said. "Don't tell Germaine, but I'm sure his rituals are getting longer."

She perched on the stool, then held out her legs, examining her swollen ankles. They did look sore.

"I'm Charlotte. A police officer with the City of London police, and I…"

The woman held up a chubby hand. "Oh, I know who you are, child," she said. "I'm Cherry."

Cherry held out her hand for Charlotte to shake.

"You're here to speak to Germaine. You need his advice on a Voodoo related case. Am I right?"

Charlotte nodded.

Cherry narrowed her eyes. "Well, that's good. Germaine is a wise man, but I will give you some advice. Don't pay any mind to anything that son of his says."

"Kwame? Why do you say that?"

"He has a chip on his shoulder. He'll tell you one hundred bad things about Voodoo but none of the good. To hear him talk, you would think he is too high and mighty for the likes of us. He may have told you he thinks it's all mumbo jumbo, but that's only because his father passed him over."

"Passed him over?" Charlotte asked.

"Kwame was supposed to be an Oracle and inherit the position after his father, but Germaine said no. He doesn't think Kwame has the skills needed to be an Oracle. Of course to hear Kwame talk, you would think he'd never wanted to be the Oracle. But that's not true."

Before Cherry could say any more, they heard footsteps in the hallway. Kwame had returned with Cherry's car keys.

"It's just outside," he said. "But you had better be quick. It's double parked."

Cherry thanked him and heaved her bulk off the kitchen stool.

"You'll remember what I said, won't you?" Cherry smiled at Charlotte.

Kwame turned and looked like he was about to ask

Charlotte what Cherry meant, when the Oracle exited the lounge with a tearful woman on his arm.

"Dad," Kwame said, attracting the Oracle's attention.

Germaine Okoro's eyes widened slightly when he saw Charlotte standing beside his son in the kitchen, but other than that his face remained impassive.

He patted the hand of the woman standing next to him, said a few quiet words and let go of her arm.

He walked towards Charlotte. "Ah, Detective Brown isn't it?"

Charlotte shook the Oracle's hand. "Yes, I'm sorry for interrupting you like this, but I wondered if you had time for a few more questions."

"Of course, of course," the Oracle said. "I always have time."

"In a few minutes, everyone will have gone," the Oracle said. "And I will be able to give you my full attention."

Charlotte nodded. "Thank you. I don't mind waiting."

She leaned against the doorjamb, watching the Oracle as he said goodbye to his followers.

The group was mainly formed of women. There was one very tall man with a slight hunchback, and there was one boy. Charlotte guessed he'd be about Francis Eze's age. Maybe twelve or thirteen. His eyes seem to fix on Charlotte, which wasn't surprising as she was quite clearly an outsider. She imagined many of the adults were probably just as curious as to why she was there.

After a few more minutes, the Oracle approached Charlotte again, touching her arm gently. "I'm sorry, detective," he said. "One of my group needs my guidance on a delicate matter, and I promised I'd see to it straight away. Perhaps I could answer your questions now, in the kitchen."

"Of course," Charlotte said.

The Oracle pushed the kitchen door closed, so they wouldn't be overheard.

"Now, tell me how I can help you?"

"I have a couple of questions," Charlotte said. "There is a name we've come across in the course of our investigation, and I hoped you might be able to shed some light on it."

The Oracle nodded. "I will do my best."

"Have you ever heard of Mr. X?"

The Oracle frowned. "I've heard some rumours about this Mr. X. More frequently in the past year, but I think it's an urban legend.

"It has been said that if you ask Mr. X for help, he will help you get rid of any enemies or obstacles in your life."

"Enemies?"

The Oracle shook his head. "It's only whispers I've heard. I don't think this is anything to do with Voodoo though."

"Can you tell me anything else about this Mr. X?"

The Oracle shook his head. "No, as I said, I don't think he really exists. I think he is something people pin their hopes on. My congregation practices the old ways, but many new offshoot religions have sprung up over the years —a combination of Voodoo and Christianity. I don't condone them."

"I see," Charlotte said. "Do you know a man called Adam Jonah?"

"No." The Oracle shook his head. "That doesn't ring any bells, I'm afraid."

Charlotte was losing hope. She was going to have to go back to Tyler with no new information.

The Oracle shot a look at the kitchen door. He was keen to get back to his congregation.

"One last question," Charlotte said. "Have you had any more thoughts regarding the identity of the flat wooden disc we showed you?"

The Oracle frowned. "Oh, yes. The disc was marked with an X, wasn't it? Are you thinking the X is related to Mr. X, like a calling card?"

Charlotte shrugged. "We really don't know. It's just a name we've come across during the investigation, and we'd like to find out more about him."

"I can ask around for you and try to find out if anyone has heard of this Mr. X. If he does exist, I'll find out who he really is."

Charlotte nodded. "Thank you."

She set down her coffee cup.

"Not at all," he said. "Let me show you out."

As the Oracle opened the kitchen door, she caught a movement out of the corner of her eye.

It was the little boy, the one who'd been staring at her since she arrived. He'd been listening at the door.

They walked down the hallway, and Charlotte turned to the Oracle. "What's his name?"

"The boy?" the Oracle asked. "That's Alfie, Alfie Adebayo. Why the interest?"

"I was just thinking how nice it is that the younger

generation is interested in your religion and culture."

The Oracle inclined his head. "It is. He usually comes with his grandmother, but Alfie came alone today." The Oracle frowned. "I try to involve the younger generation as much as possible. It's nice to have the old traditions continued, and for people to remain in touch with their cultural roots."

Charlotte said goodbye to the Oracle and set off along the street in the direction of the underground. She hadn't had much luck in identifying Mr. X, but hopefully the Oracle could find out more.

Charlotte stepped off the pavement as a young mum with a double buggy strode towards her. Charlotte smiled as she passed, but the woman stared back, her face blank.

Suit yourself, Charlotte thought and stepped back onto the pavement. The air was crisp. A proper autumnal day. The mist had cleared, but the plummeting temperatures signalled winter was waiting in the wings.

Charlotte had just reached the corner of Queen Street, when she felt a sharp tug on her jacket.

The shock made her gasp.

She whirled around with her hands raised, and she saw the little boy Alfie Adebayo behind her.

He wore a hooded parka. The hood was pulled so low, she wouldn't have recognised him from a distance. *Was he hiding from someone?*

She dismissed the thought as quickly as it came to her. She was imagining things. Most kids wore hoodies these days, and it was cold. It made sense that he'd have his hood pulled up, so why did it trigger alarm bells?

As her heartbeat returned to normal, Charlotte took a deep breath. "You shouldn't creep up on people like that."

The boy looked more terrified than she did. He stared up at her with huge brown eyes.

"It's Alfie isn't it?" she asked. "I'm Charlotte."

He nodded. "Are you a police officer?" he asked.

"Yes, that's right."

She waited to see what else he would say.

The boy licked his lips and blinked. He looked over his shoulder to make sure they were alone, then he took a step closer to Charlotte and whispered, "I heard you."

Charlotte frowned. "You heard me? What did you hear?"

"You want to find out about Mr. X," Alfie said. His voice trembled ever so slightly.

Charlotte nodded. "Do you know who he is?"

The boy looked as if he might run away at any moment, which was the last thing Charlotte wanted.

She leaned down towards him, but he shrank away.

As someone crossed the street ahead of them, a group of pigeons took off, flapping their wings, narrowly missing Charlotte's head as they powered their plump bodies upwards. Alfie jumped.

"It's okay, Alfie. You can tell me," she said.

Alfie swallowed and looked at her for a long time without saying anything, as though he was weighing her up.

Then he nodded.

"I can take you to someone who knows him," he said.

CHAPTER TWENTY-SIX

CHARLOTTE STARTED TO FEEL A little uneasy as she followed Alfie through the twisting alleys that snaked between the blocks of flats on the Towers Estate.

The alleyways were dark, and when you entered, you couldn't see all the way to the exit. Charlotte didn't like that.

She pulled out her mobile and typed a quick text to Mackinnon, telling him where she was.

Better safe than sorry.

Charlotte blinked as they exited an alleyway into a huge open square surrounded by tower blocks.

The ground was a huge mass of crumbling concrete.

"It's this one," Alfie said, nodding to the entrance of Manor Park House.

Alfie stood by the door and looked back at Charlotte.

Manor Park House had seen better days. It was the perfect example touted by those who campaigned to have the Towers Estate demolished. The light grey exterior was streaked with black marks. Some of the ground floor and first floor windows had been boarded up, and those that weren't were smeared with grime.

"Is this it?" Charlotte asked. "Does Mr. X live here?

Alfie hesitated and then shook his head.

Charlotte frowned. It wasn't easy getting information out of this kid.

She tried again.

"Is there someone who lives here who can tell me about Mr. X?"

Alfie nodded, turned and disappeared into the dark entrance. Charlotte suppressed the uneasy feeling that had grown as she walked through the estate and followed him.

Inside the dim hallway, Charlotte wrinkled her nose. It smelled of old boiled vegetables. She followed Alfie up the stairs, counting the floors as they went.

They exited the stairwell on the third floor, and Alfie led her along the landing to the flat at the far end.

There was a coarse brown mat outside the front door, with the word welcome dyed on it. Charlotte didn't feel particularly welcome.

She thought perhaps she shouldn't have come alone. She could have asked Mackinnon to tag along, but he was busy. The whole team was, and this could end up being a wild goose chase.

Charlotte lifted up her hand to ring the doorbell when Alfie surprised her by pulling a set of keys out of his pocket and opening the door.

"You live here?" Charlotte asked.

Alfie nodded and beckoned for Charlotte to follow him inside.

"Is that you Alfie?" Charlotte heard a woman's voice call from inside the flat, and a moment later a woman appeared in the hallway.

She was short, dark-skinned with tight curls around her face, and she wore huge dangly gold earrings.

"What's this, Alfie?" the woman asked, immediately defensive. "Who are you?"

Before Charlotte could answer, Alfie piped up. "She wants to know about Mr. X."

The woman's face relaxed and she smiled.

"Oh, I see," she said. "You need a little help from Mr. X."

She held out a long, red-painted talon and curled her finger to beckon Charlotte towards her.

"Come in here. We'll be more comfortable," she said and opened the door to her right.

Charlotte wasn't exactly sure why she hadn't introduced herself and shown her ID immediately, but she had a feeling she would find out more if she didn't admit to being a police officer.

The room they walked into was dark. The curtains had been closed, and a candle flickered in the corner giving the whole room an eerie light.

"Can we turn the light on?" Charlotte asked.

"No," the woman said. "We work by candlelight."

She shut the door, leaving Alfie outside in the hall, and pulled out a chair beside a small table, then indicated for Charlotte to take the other chair, which she did.

The table was scattered with tiny shells, and there was a small dish that contained something that looked like a blackened, shrivelled chicken's head.

Charlotte looked away.

It was warm in here, and the scent of incense was strong.

The woman leaned forward, placing her forearms on the table.

"Why do you need help from Mr. X?" she asked.

Charlotte shifted uncomfortably under the woman's gaze. She didn't like the way she was staring at her, like she could see right inside her, and see all her secrets.

Charlotte looked down at one of the shells and reached out to touch it.

"Don't touch," the women said. "You'll disturb the spirits. Only I can touch the shells."

She moved the shells away and out of Charlotte's reach.

"You want help from Mr. X," the woman stated. "You want him to get rid of a problem for you. That is fine. We can help you. All I need is a name."

She lifted the bowl containing the chicken's head and took a small scrap of paper from underneath. She pushed it across the table towards Charlotte, and took a pen from behind her ear and placed that on top of the paper.

"Name?" she said.

Charlotte swallowed. She wasn't sure how long she could keep this up without explaining to the woman who she really was.

"I'm not really sure about this," Charlotte said. "Can you explain the process to me?"

The woman's eyes narrowed. "You don't need to worry about the process. The spirits take care of that. Mr. X will see that the spirits hear your prayers."

Charlotte picked up the pen, pressing the nib hard against the piece of paper.

She was surprised when a name came unbidden into her mind, and she thought for just a split second how nice it would be to write down the name of her abusive ex-boyfriend, but a second later, she put down the pen.

"I'm not really sure. I don't want anyone to get hurt."

The woman sucked in a breath and shook her head so hard that the curls slapped her cheeks.

"Are you wasting my time, girl?" she asked. "Mr. X has lots of people wanting his help. He is a busy man, so do you want his help, or not?"

"What will he do?"

"Mr. X will make sure the spirits hear your prayers," the woman said again. "I need a name and address and your problems will be over."

"How much does it cost?"

"If you give me five-thousand pounds, the spirits will hear your prayers."

"That's a lot of money," Charlotte said. "I don't even know your name. How do I know you won't just run off with my money?"

The woman sucked in a breath and held a hand to her chest, as if she was terribly offended that Charlotte could suggest such a thing.

Charlotte wiped her sweaty palms on her trousers. The incense was making her feel light-headed.

"If it makes you feel better, my name is Erika. This is my home." She gestured around the dark room. "How could I run off with your money? I live here. You'd soon track me down."

"So, you're saying, I just need to trust you?"

"That depends on how badly you want to get rid of your problem," the woman said.

She leaned so close Charlotte could smell the coffee on her breath.

Charlotte was regretting coming here alone. She should have shown her ID as soon as she'd entered the flat. It wasn't as if she'd be able to use any of this information as evidence. Still, something kept her from reaching for her ID. If Erika would just tell her a little more, at least they'd have a better idea of what they were up against.

"Who is Mr. X?" Charlotte asked.

"He is the righter of wrongs," the woman said. "He is justice where there is injustice. He is the spirit guide."

Charlotte wasn't getting anywhere. The woman was talking in riddles. Charlotte put down the pen and reached into her pocket.

She held up her ID.

The woman took a while to realise what it was. She frowned at the warrant card. It was dark in here and Erika obviously found it difficult to read.

Suddenly, she leaned forward and snatched it from Charlotte's hand.

Erika's eyes widened as she scanned the ID.

She slapped it on the tabletop.

"This is entrapment," she snarled. "You can't just come into my house like this!"

Charlotte ignored the woman's protestations and stood up.

Riled the woman stood, too, and said, "You don't know who you are messing with."

Charlotte picked up her ID. "Well, I'm hoping you're going to tell me exactly who I'm messing with."

The woman shook her head. "You don't understand. He's too powerful. He's got…"

"You'll have plenty of time to tell me all about him when we get back to the station," Charlotte said and walked over to open the door.

"Where's Alfie?" Charlotte asked, turning back to Erika.

The woman scowled. "My nephew's probably gone out again by now. He's never home. He's always getting into trouble. He brought you here, didn't he? The little bastard."

Charlotte beckoned the woman to get up. "Come on," she said, reaching in her pocket for her mobile phone. "I'll get one of my colleagues to give us a lift to the station."

CHAPTER TWENTY-SEVEN

HELEN ROOKE STEPPED INSIDE THE lift. Her heart was hammering furiously, and her hand shook slightly as she reached out to press the button for the third floor of the swanky, riverside apartment block.

She had an hour until she was due to start her shift as a nurse at the local hospital. She didn't want to be late, but she had to do this first. She'd been worrying about it all morning.

She couldn't put it off any longer.

As the lift came to a shuddering halt, and the doors squeaked open, Helen felt a sense of dread in the pit of her stomach.

No turning back now, she told herself. It's better to know than to live constantly worrying about it.

She stepped out into the communal hallway and turned left, fumbling in her bag for the keys.

She rarely ever used the keys. Her boyfriend, Mark

Fleming, had given her a set to his flat over a year ago, but she still always knocked. Today things were different.

Today she didn't want Mark to know she was coming. That was the whole point.

She stopped outside the door to Mark's flat and listened intently.

She wasn't sure exactly what she was expecting to hear. Perhaps Mark laughing, and a female high-pitched voice giggling alongside him, but there was nothing.

Through the small square window in the door, she could see that the lights were on inside the flat.

She raised the key and hesitated. Should she really be doing this? Maybe it was better not to know. Maybe she was being paranoid like Mark said.

Lately he had been so busy he hadn't had any time for Helen.

He said it was because he'd just started up a new position and it was very stressful. His job was to rework the corporate structure of companies and that involved laying people off.

He'd rolled his eyes at Helen's questions, and explained, in his patronising tone, that he'd started a new job with lots of responsibilities so, of course, he would be busy. Of course, Helen couldn't possibly understand, he'd said, what with her *only* being a nurse.

Helen had almost given him a slap and stormed out there and then. *Only a nurse?* She'd like to see him dealing with blood and vomit on a daily basis.

Having a patient's life in her hands was far more

responsibility than Mark could even dream of as far as she was concerned.

But he'd been fobbing her off. Helen understood that a new job would keep him busy, but what she didn't understand was all the secrecy. All of a sudden, he'd put a special password on his phone. He got annoyed if she asked to use his iPad, and last week, he'd shouted at her when she'd answered his phone while he'd been in the shower.

She'd suspected Mark of having an affair for months now. And today was the day, one way or another, that she would find out for sure.

Helen adjusted the handbag strap on her shoulder and lifted her chin. There was no point hiding her head in the sand. She had to confront him and find out the truth.

Helen put the key in the lock and turned it, pushing the door forward. She paused again in the doorway, listening out for tell-tale signs, but there was nothing.

She closed the door quietly behind her, then bent over to take off her heels.

Mark was very particular about his flat. He wouldn't want her heels damaging his polished oak floorboards.

And it suited her purpose today. She didn't want the click clack of her heels to give her away before she was ready.

She moved forward, and the floorboards creaked under her feet. That was the only sound in the flat.

She frowned. It was very strange that there wasn't any music playing, and the TV wasn't on.

Mark wasn't exactly a quiet person. He was usually humming out of tune or whistling along to music as he worked. That was something that had always irritated Helen. He was never quiet.

She stood in the hallway, straining to hear, but there was no noise at all.

Perhaps he wasn't here after all. Great. She built herself up for nothing.

Helen walked forward. While she was here, she may as well check Mark's bedroom.

Outside the bedroom door, she paused again. What if Mark was in there with another woman? Perhaps they'd fallen asleep and that was why it was so quiet.

Her heart was beating like a drum, and her mouth felt cracked and dry. She was scared. Whatever she found beyond this door would affect the rest of her life.

She had to pull herself together. If he was cheating on her, then she deserved to know, and she'd make sure he didn't have the chance to do it again.

She took a deep breath and pushed at the door. As it opened, Helen saw the crumpled sheets strewn over Mark's unmade bed in the middle of the room.

She bit down on her lip. It doesn't mean anything, she told herself. An unmade bed wasn't proof.

She felt tears prick the corner of her eyes. Mark was a tidy person. Everything had to be in its proper place in his flat, and she'd never known him not to make the bed so that meant…

Helen turned away, furious now, sure she had the evidence she needed. She didn't need someone like that. He was a lying, cheating scumbag. She was better off without him, and she was going to tell him so.

She left the bedroom, stormed up the hallway and entered the main living area that Mark had set out as a sitting room as well as his study.

As soon as she stepped inside the room, she smelt the metallic tang of blood. She felt her throat close up.

On the floor, in front of the brown three-seater sofa, Mark lay face-down on the floor, his arms and legs spreadeagled.

He wore jeans, but his top half was bare, and two thick red gashes crossed his back, flaying the skin.

For a moment, Helen couldn't move. Her feet were rooted to the floor.

Somewhere in the back of her mind, her medical training kicked in, and she leaned down to try and help Mark. She reached out a hand only to snatch it back.

What if whoever did this was still here?

The blood was already darkening, turning a rusty brown. That meant he'd been dead a while.

That was good. It meant the killer probably wasn't still here.

Helen tottered round, spinning in a circle, suddenly scared that she wasn't alone, that the killer was here, in the flat, waiting for its next victim.

Acting on base instinct, Helen ran faster than she'd ever run before, bumping against the walls as she bolted down the hallway and out of the front door.

She didn't bother with the lift this time. Instead, she scrambled down the stairs, jumping them two at a time.

She slipped at the bottom and went down hard on one

knee, which sent a shockwave all the way through her body.

She used the handrail to heave herself up and limped towards the exit.

When she reached the outside, she took a ragged breath. She staggered for a moment in the hazy October sunlight, looking around. There were cars stuck in traffic on the road. A woman walked past with a little boy. A bus had stopped just a few yards away, dropping off two passengers.

Everything was going on as normal. No one had any idea of the horrors that had happened upstairs.

Helen looked behind her as the block of flats loomed large and she shivered. She fumbled in her bag for her mobile phone. Her shaking fingers had trouble typing out 999.

"Hello," Helen said. "I need the police. It's my boyfriend, Mark Fleming. He's been murdered."

CHAPTER TWENTY-EIGHT

THEY GOT THE NEWS ABOUT the next victim, Mark Fleming, from the Metropolitan police. He'd been found dead in his flat by his girlfriend.

It was the same M.O. in some ways as the two early murders. But Mark Fleming obviously moved in different social circles.

Collins knew that three bedroom apartments around the Quays sold for close to a million pounds.

Collins frowned. There had to be some link between the victims. There usually was. Genuine random killings were rare. Even serial killers, who were believed to pick their victims randomly, tended to have a type. The victims often had similar professions or lived in certain areas.

Everything in life had a pattern if you looked closely enough, and murders were no exception.

All Collins and the team had to do was find the pattern.

Collins looked across the table. Helen Rooke sat nursing

a cup of coffee, looking completely shattered. Collins's heart went out to her. She'd just had a hell of a shock.

She had already been through questioning with the Met officers, so Collins had been trying to take it easy.

Helen Rooke stared down numbly at her coffee.

Collins pushed two A5 glossy head shots towards her. "Do you recognise them?"

Helen stared vacantly at the pictures of Francis Eze and Adam Jonah.

She looked for so long that Collins began to think that she recognised them.

But then she looked up at him, and he realised she was finding it hard to concentrate on the here and now. Her mind was back in the flat. She didn't see the faces of Francis Eze or Adam Jonah. She was seeing the blood-soaked body of her boyfriend.

Collins would have preferred to wait and give the woman time to grieve, but they didn't have the time. She could have essential information.

"Do either of them look familiar?" Collins prompted.

Helen stared down at the photographs again, then shook her head

"I'm sorry. No, they don't."

"Can you think of anyone who might have wanted to hurt your boyfriend?"

Helen blinked. "Quite a few people actually."

Helen ran a hand through her hair. "He'd just started a new position," she said. "His job was to restructure a multi-national company. He fired quite a few of the employees.

They weren't happy about it, but it wasn't Mark's fault. He was just doing his job."

Collins nodded. This was good. They could look into this. "Can you give me the name of the company and any of the employees Mark mentioned?"

Helen nodded and recited a short list of names for Collins.

"Anything else you can think of? Anyone else he'd had a run-in with lately?"

Her eyes teared up, and she leaned across the table, staring up at Collins.

"I didn't mention it to the other officers because I was worried about how it would seem, but I thought he was cheating on me," she said. "That's why I'd gone there today. I needed to find out the truth... But I didn't expect to find that."

Helen shivered.

"Can I get you another drink?" Collins asked.

Helen looked down at her coffee cup, which was still two-thirds full.

"That must have gone cold by now," Collins said.

Helen shook her head. "Thank you, but I don't want anything," she said.

"If he was seeing someone else," Collins said, wary of the dangerous ground he was treading on, "do you have any idea who it might be?"

Helen shrugged. "No idea."

Collins took a sip of his own coffee. Perhaps Mark Fleming's mistress got fed up with waiting...

"I suppose you're going to look into his personal life now, aren't you? You'll find all sorts of things."

Collins nodded. "We need to do that to find out who killed him."

Helen nodded. "I see," she said.

Collins didn't want to say any more, but he knew the Met officers were already all over Mark Fleming's personal correspondence. They had his computer and his phone, and they'd found out he was indeed having an affair, with a woman called Lia Gold.

It was a hell of a thing to get over after finding her boyfriend's body like that, but Collins hoped Helen would be all right.

She seemed like a strong woman underneath the shock, and she definitely didn't deserve to be treated the way Mark Fleming had treated her.

Collins hoped Helen Rooke could eventually get over this, find herself some happiness and meet someone who deserved her. Because Mark Fleming certainly hadn't.

CHAPTER TWENTY-NINE

"HER NAME IS ERIKA DARAGO," Charlotte said, passing Mackinnon the file. They stood by the vending machines on the second floor of Wood Street Station.

"Is she definitely involved?"

Charlotte nodded. "If you ask me, she's in it up to her neck."

"Have they tracked down the boy yet?" Mackinnon asked, feeding a pound coin into the machine.

Charlotte shook her head. She was getting really worried about Alfie.

"No," she said and sighed. "He's only twelve. He's a friend of Francis. Can you imagine how scared he must be right now? Rosialie has spoken to Francis's parents just in case Alfie goes to them.

"We've got an alert out for him, so if any units spot him, they'll contact us straight away. And I've called social services."

Mackinnon nodded. "Has Erika Darago said anything?"

"She's been saying a whole lot of things," Charlotte said. "Mainly just mouthing off. Tyler's leaving her to cool down at the moment. He's going in for a second round soon. I'm not sure who he wants in there with him, but it's certainly not me. The lovely Erika is after my blood."

Mackinnon nodded and unwrapped a chocolate bar, offering a piece to Charlotte.

She turned him down. Charlotte must be worried. He'd never known her to turn down chocolate before.

Mackinnon left Charlotte on the second floor and went in search of DI Tyler. He found Tyler in the incident room, his head bent over the desk, furiously scribbling on a piece of paper.

"What's she told us so far?" Mackinnon asked.

Tyler looked up and exhaled deeply. "She has said she doesn't know the identity of our Mr. X. According to Erika Darago, she leaves notes for him in a mailbox in an abandoned office building. That's how they communicate. She's never actually met him."

Tyler nodded towards DC Webb's desk. "Webb is checking who owns the abandoned offices, and there are cameras across the street on one of the other buildings, so hopefully we can get some footage."

DC Webb had his eyes fixed on his computer screen, the faint blue light from the screen reflected on his face made him look washed out.

"They still haven't found Alfie Adebayo," Mackinnon said. "Do you think he's in danger?"

Tyler sighed and put down his pen. "I've got no idea," he said. "But I hope the boy is somewhere safe. He is a key witness, and if our killer is smart enough to realise that…"

Tyler trailed off without saying the obvious. Mackinnon knew what he meant. As much as they wanted to find Alfie and get him to talk, there was someone else out there who would like to find Alfie to silence him.

They were interrupted by DC Webb swearing loudly at his computer. He looked up at them.

"It's a dead end," he said. "The building's owned by a company. They have plans to redevelop it in the next couple of months. They can give us a list of names of people with keys and there's a security company who visits a couple of times a day, but I'm not hopeful we will get anything from the list. I reckon our Mr. X has just picked out an abandoned building to use for his purpose."

Tyler nodded. "Okay, but we don't know they're not involved. Could be that someone at the company or someone working security detail knows something. So, we need to check every name you have on that list."

DC Webb looked down at his list. "Right," he said. Shoulders slumped, he turned back towards his computer.

The phone on Tyler's desk rang and he snatched it up.

"DI Tyler," he barked into it.

"Yes, sir," Tyler said. "Of course, sir." Mackinnon could tell by the change in Tyler's tone that he was talking to DCI Brookbank.

As DI Tyler was on the phone, he didn't notice Evie Charlesworth come up behind Mackinnon.

"We've managed to get some footage of the building," she said.

Mackinnon felt hope rise in his chest.

"Can you see Erika Darago?"

"Yes, we can see Erika Darago. We can't see where she leaves the note, obviously, but we can see her going into the building."

Mackinnon nodded. "Good." Then he asked the million-dollar question. "But can we see anyone picking it up?"

It turned out there was somebody entering the building a short time after Erika Darago left. But they couldn't identify the figure. They couldn't even tell if it was male or female.

Mackinnon watched the replay. Ten minutes after Erika Darago left the office block, a dark figure, wearing a hooded coat, arrived at the front of the building, ducking beneath the no-entry tape and entering the double doors.

Tyler, Mackinnon and Webb crowded round the monitor, eager to see whether they would get a better picture when the figure came out of the building, but they were out of luck. The figure exited the building. With the big coat the suspect wore and the way the hood was pulled down low, there was no chance of an ID.

"Shit," Tyler said. "Do you think we can enhance that?"

"Not a chance," DC Webb said. "You won't get anything better than that. It would be a waste of time trying to enhance it."

Tyler swore again, and Mackinnon felt his phone vibrate in his pocket. He pulled it out, and seeing it was a number he didn't recognise, he excused himself and walked back over to his desk in the incident room.

"DS Mackinnon," he said.

A female voice answered. "This is Lucy," she said. "Lucy Sampson. I'm the nanny for Joy Barter."

"Hi, Lucy. How can I help?" Mackinnon asked and waited for her to continue. He knew the nanny had wanted to tell them something the last time they had visited Joy Barter's house.

"I wondered if you could come and see me," she said. "I've got some information you might be interested in."

"Of course," Mackinnon said. "Should I come to the house?"

"No," Lucy Sampson said, urgently. "Don't do that. Can you meet me in Holland Park? At the children's play area?

"I'm going to take Thomas there in half an hour and I don't really want Mrs. Barter to find out. You don't have to tell her, do you?"

Mackinnon assured her that he wouldn't tell Joy Barter about their meeting, and Lucy gave him instructions on how to find the children's play area.

After he'd ended the call to Lucy Sampson, he headed back to see Tyler.

"I've got a job for you, Mackinnon," Tyler said. "I want you to go and check out this building where Erika Darago and our so-called Mr. X were exchanging their notes."

Mackinnon grimaced. "I've just had a call from Joy Barter's nanny, Lucy Sampson. She says she has some information, and I told her I'd meet her in half an hour."

Annoyance played over Tyler's face for a moment, then

he said, "All right, fine. You go. I'll get Collins and Charlotte to check out the building."

Mackinnon nodded and headed out, grabbing his coat on the way.

It took Mackinnon thirty minutes to get there. The sun was setting, and the day was cold. It wasn't really the weather for enjoying an adventure playground, so Mackinnon wasn't surprised there was no one else in the play area apart from Lucy Sampson and Joy Barter's little boy, Thomas.

Thomas gave Mackinnon a cheeky smile from the top of the slide.

Lucy Sampson was seated on a wooden bench beside the slide. She stood up and waved at Mackinnon, then she looked past him, as though she was expecting Joy Barter to sneak up on her at any moment.

Mackinnon made his way over to the bench and they both sat down.

"I'm glad you called," Mackinnon said.

Lucy bit her lip. "I'm not sure it was the right thing to do," she said. "But I just want to do what's best for him."

She looked at Thomas who had arrived at the bottom of the shiny, metal slide and was running back for another go.

"It's good that he's got someone like you to look out for him," Mackinnon said.

Lucy took a deep breath then she said, "I called you about something that happened a week ago. It's probably nothing important. It just seemed really strange at the time. You see, Thomas goes to nursery three times a week, and I normally have the car to pick him up. It's too far for him to walk, and it was pouring with rain."

Lucy paused, her eyes seeking out Thomas. Once she saw he was safe and climbing the slide, she continued, "The thing is, Mrs. Barter said that I couldn't use the car. She said she needed it that day, so I asked if I could take Thomas in a taxi and she told me I was being very lazy."

Mackinnon nodded and waited for her to continue.

"In the end she got all huffy. She said she didn't want her little boy in a taxi filled with germs." Lucy rolled her eyes. "She's got a thing about public transport. So in the end, she said that she would pick us up and that she might be a few minutes late."

"And was she?" Mackinnon asked.

Lucy shook her head. "No, that's the funny thing, she was there early, but she said she had to go somewhere afterwards and we would have to wait for her in the car."

"She parked up in a shady part of town. That's what seemed so weird. It wasn't the type of place she'd normally go," Lucy said.

"I see," Mackinnon said. "Do you remember the name of the road?"

Lucy Sampson frowned. "I don't remember the name of the road," she said. "But I knew we were in the Towers Estate. I don't know the door number she went to because it was a block of flats. But I remember the block of flats was called Manor Park House."

Mackinnon nodded, his mind whirring. *Manor Park House.* That was the address of Erika Darago.

"And what day was that?" Mackinnon asked.

"It was Wednesday," Lucy said.

Mackinnon watched the little boy, who had now moved on to the swings.

Wednesday… not long after Joy Barter had withdrawn five thousand pounds in cash.

How could that possibly be a coincidence?

CHAPTER THIRTY

"WHAT DO YOU THINK WE'LL find?" Charlotte asked, as Collins drove towards the East End.

"God knows," Collins said. "But there has to be something. The net is closing in on our elusive Mr. X."

Collins indicated and took the next right. "You know, I feel a bit of an idiot calling him Mr. X. I mean, what sort of a name is that?"

Charlotte shrugged, loosening her scarf. The car's heaters were blasting out hot air. "Hopefully we'll have his real name soon."

Collins slowed the car as they approached the abandoned office block. The building used to be owned by CO Insurance, but it had ceased trading almost two years ago. The land had been purchased by a developer, but the refurbishment work hadn't started yet.

Charlotte climbed out of the car and slammed the door. She stared up at the building.

Grey cladding covered the front, interspersed with small square windows. It was nothing like the office blocks built today, with their huge windows, letting in plenty of light.

Working at CO Insurance must have been a dark, gloomy experience.

The building was surrounded by plywood boards. To the right, Charlotte spotted the entrance. A thick, metal chain and padlock had secured the gate once, but it had been cut. The chain dangled by the entrance.

Charlotte raised an eyebrow and turned to Collins, who was locking the car.

"Don't think much of their so-called security."

She walked to the gate and inspected the chain. "It's been cut right through. A clean cut. Probably bolt-cutters."

Collins leaned over her shoulder. "Interesting. I'm going to go around the perimeter first, check there isn't another entrance or exit."

"Okay." Charlotte zipped up her coat and pulled a pair of latex gloves from her pocket. "I'll go in. Meet you in there."

Collins nodded and set off around the perimeter.

The gate creaked on its hinges as Charlotte pulled it open. It didn't open very far before the bottom of the gate wedged itself against a mound in the uneven floor. Great design. She squeezed through the small gap.

Behind the wooden boards, the air seemed unnaturally still. Charlotte shivered. It's just because the boards are blocking the wind, she told herself, moving forwards.

Directly in front of her was what looked like an old service doorway. All that remained of the old wooden door was a collection of splinters and some peeling blue paint. The door had been shattered.

Someone had been very determined to get in.

Charlotte walked towards the entrance. Behind the broken door, the entrance to the building was pitch black. She took a deep breath and pulled her torch from the inside pocket of her jacket.

She flicked the switch, testing the light. The narrow beam of light flitted from right to left as she tried to see inside the building.

There were a few old ceiling tiles scattered over the floor, but it didn't look dangerous or unstable.

Charlotte stepped inside.

As she walked further inside the building the temperature seemed to get even colder. It was a struggle to stop her teeth chattering.

Ahead of her was a staircase and on her left there was an open doorway.

Which way first?

They would need to search the whole property eventually, but the sooner they got their hands on some evidence, the better.

Charlotte chose to climb the staircase. The steps were rickety, and she had to take care not to stumble on yet more ceiling tiles.

Halfway up the stairs, Charlotte thought she heard laughter. She stood still, listening, but she didn't hear it again.

She was surrounded by darkness now, the light from the doorway where she'd entered had faded to nothing.

"Collins?" she called out into the darkness. "Is that you?"

There was no answer.

Just the wind whistling, Charlotte told herself, and resumed climbing the stairs.

It was so cold. Charlotte rubbed her nose and sniffed. It smelled bad, too. Mould, mildew and neglect.

A long drawn out creak sounded above her. It sounded like someone was up there. She ran up the rest of the stairs, praying that she wouldn't trip as the beam of her torch bounced off the walls.

At the top of the stairs, there was a large rectangular landing. Charlotte paused and spun round in a circle. Which way had the noise come from?

It was so cold she could see her breath in front of her.

There was a door on each side of the landing. She moved to her left, her torch pointing at the door.

Charlotte blinked. Had the door handle turned? When she shone the light back on the handle, it hadn't changed position, but she could have sworn she saw movement...

She pushed the door open and burst into the room. It wasn't as dark in here. The remaining hazy light from the setting sun filtered in through the grimy small windows.

It was a huge room that had probably once held row upon row of office staff.

Charlotte moved forward. It was nice to be able to see further than the end of her nose, but she kept the torch switched on.

Charlotte walked slowly around the room, shining her torch into the corners. She couldn't see anything of interest, so she decided to head to the doorway at the far end of the room.

For some reason, the base of the door seemed to glow. Was there a light in there? Was it Collins?

Charlotte was about to call out when a shadow flitted past the other side of the door, temporarily blocking the light.

Charlotte gripped her torch. It's Collins, she told herself. It must be.

She walked towards the door slowly and put her hand on the old-fashioned brass door knob. The handle was freezing.

She bit down on her lip and pushed open the door. She waited a moment before entering the room, listening.

She could hear the traffic on the street below. But nothing else.

Charlotte stepped inside the room. It was almost identical to the one she'd left. She shone her torch on the floor, and walked on, avoiding the mouse droppings.

Another long drawn out creak had Charlotte spinning around. The room was still empty, but the door she had just walked through was now closed.

She had left it open, hadn't she?

Charlotte swallowed and swung the torch around the room again to make sure she was alone.

The torch light found an object in the middle of the room.

That was funny. It almost looked like a red pouch.

As she moved closer, she saw that was exactly what it was.

Charlotte placed the torch on the ground and crouched down. She picked up the pouch with her gloved hands. Inside were at least ten flat wooden discs, all with an X engraved on one side.

Charlotte put the pouch back down on the floor. She felt sick. That had been left here for them to find.

She took a deep breath, and as she stood up, her mobile emitted a shrill ring, making her jump.

"Jesus," she said, pressing a hand to her chest.

She answered the phone. It was Collins.

"I've found something," Charlotte said. "You'd better come and look."

CHAPTER THIRTY-ONE

BY THE TIME MACKINNON, CHARLOTTE and Collins returned to Wood Street Station, Erika Darago had got herself a solicitor.

"Great," Charlotte said. "She might not have been telling us what we wanted to know, but at least, she was talking. Now we won't get anything out of her."

Mackinnon pulled over a chair and sat down beside Charlotte. Collins perched on the edge of her desk. They had just returned from briefing Tyler and the rest of the team on what Collins and Charlotte had discovered at the abandoned office block and the information Mackinnon had learned from Joy Barter's nanny.

When things started really moving on a case, it was tempting to delay the briefings and push on. But that was a bad idea. The whole team needed to have the latest developments, otherwise things could easily slip through the gaps.

"We're closing in on him," Collins said. "We know where he has been working, and we've got his accomplice, Erika Darago, in custody."

Charlotte sighed. "I don't know, Nick. He left those discs there for us to find. And we still don't know where Francis Eze and Adam Jonah were killed. There was no evidence of blood at the abandoned building, and there should have been."

"When we left, the building was crawling with SOCOs. If there's any evidence there they will find it," Collins said, but he didn't sound very confident.

"We've got a link between Joy Barter and Erika Darago. Lucy Sampson said she waited for Joy outside Erika Darago's block of flats," Mackinnon said. "I'm willing to bet that Joy Barter's five grand in cash went to Mr. X via Erika Darago."

Charlotte shook her head. "A payment for killing poor Adam Jonah. Of course, Erika Darago never admitted as much. Instead, she promised Mr. X would make sure the spirits got rid of the obstacles in my life."

Mackinnon leaned back in his chair and stared up at the fluorescent ceiling lights. "Five grand is not much for a life is it."

"We've got loads of links to Mr. X. It keeps coming back to him," Collins said. "But all of that is useless when we don't know who he is. I mean, Erika Darago tells us she never met him and only kept in contact through the notes left in the abandoned offices, but do we really believe that?"

DI Tyler entered the incident room and clapped his hands to get everyone's attention.

"All right, listen up," he said. "I've just been on the phone to DI Miller at the Met. They got a prime suspect for the latest victim, Mark Fleming."

Everyone in the room stopped what they were doing. Tyler glanced down at his notes.

"The suspect's name is Eric Madison. He apparently took his dismissal very seriously. He's been cautioned for leaving a bag of faeces in Fleming's car. He's also left threatening letters for Fleming, pushed under his front door. Madison's fingerprints are all over them, so we're not dealing with a master criminal here. DI Miller is sure Madison is going to be our weak link in the chain.

"I've sent DI Miller a headshot of Erika Darago. If he recognises her and is prepared to give evidence to the fact he paid her to organise the Fleming murder, it will be a great leap forward."

There were murmurs of excitement around the room, but Tyler raised a hand.

"It's progress," he said. "But it's not enough. We need to find Mr. X. Erika Darago was just a go-between. We've got a serial killer for hire out there, and we need to find him fast."

Tyler nodded. "All right, what are you all standing around for? Get back to work."

Mackinnon smirked. Typical Tyler.

"Sir?" Charlotte spoke up just as Tyler was turning to leave the room. "Is there any news on Alfie Adebayo?"

Tyler shook his head. His grey hair flopped forward over his forehead and he shoved it back with one hand. "Not yet."

Charlotte nodded and turned her attention back to her computer monitor, chewing on a thumbnail.

She was nervous and had good reason to be, Mackinnon thought. There was a good chance Alfie may have seen Joy Barter and Eric Madison coming to the flat to talk to his aunt.

What Mackinnon couldn't understand was how all this related to Francis Eze. Who would hire a hit on a twelve-year old boy?

Mackinnon looked at his watch. He should be knocking off duty in ten minutes, but he didn't imagine he'd be getting home anytime soon. He smothered a yawn.

"I'm going to go to the interview suite," Mackinnon said. "They should be starting to interview Erika Darago again soon."

"I'll come with you," Charlotte said.

By the time they got to the interview suite, the interview was already well underway. Charlotte led the way into the dimly lit viewing area and Mackinnon closed the door behind them. They stood behind the one-way glass.

In the interview room, Erika Darago looked wild. Her hair, which had been so carefully curled earlier, was now in disarray, and her eye makeup was smudged, making her eyes look even bigger.

"It's the spirits," she said. "Not me. It's not murder if I don't do it, is it?"

"Conspiracy to murder at the very least," DCI Brookbank said. "Especially the boy. Prison is not a very nice experience for child killers."

Erika Darago screeched at him and tugged at her hair. "I

don't know anything about a child. I just took down names, but none of them were children."

Brookbank shrugged. "We might be more inclined to believe you if you had a list of the names."

Erika Darago stared at the DCI. "You want a list?"

"We want the names," Brookbank said, almost growling.

For a long moment, no one said anything. Mackinnon realised he was holding his breath.

Erika Darago turned to her solicitor, who whispered in her ear.

The solicitor adjusted his tie and sat up a little straighter in his chair. "My client would like to talk about doing a deal."

"I bet she would," Charlotte said. She stood next to Mackinnon, her hands clenched in fists at her sides. "She's a nasty piece of work."

Mackinnon stared in at Erika Darago. The bright lights of the interview room reflected off the sheen of sweat on her forehead.

"Do you think she is lying?" Mackinnon asked. "Do you think she really knows who Mr. X is?"

Charlotte shrugged. "It could be her husband, Remi Darago. She could be protecting him."

"Without knowing the identity of Mr. X, we don't have the most important piece of the puzzle," Mackinnon said. "We need to know who this Mr. X is."

Charlotte shrugged. "Remi Darago didn't turn up for his afternoon shift at the shop where he works. He's gone AWOL. We've got an APW out on him now."

Inside the interview room, Erika Darago was muttering to her solicitor, whispering in his ear.

"Do you two need some time alone?" Brookbank's tone was cutting.

The solicitor swallowed, and his prominent Adam's apple bobbed up and down.

"No, thank you," the solicitor said. "My client is prepared to give you the list."

"Where is it?" Brookbank asked.

Officers and the SOCO team had been through Erika and Remi Darago's flat with a fine tooth comb, but they hadn't found a list.

Erika Darago lifted her index finger to the side of her head and tapped on her temple with a long red fingernail.

"It's all up here," she said. Her eyes narrowed as she smiled.

That was good. If she'd memorised the list, hopefully that meant it was short. They'd found three bodies, Francis Eze, Adam Jonah and Mark Fleming, but that didn't mean there weren't more out there.

Brookbank pushed a sheet of blank A4 paper across the desk. He uncapped a pen and set it down on top of the paper. "Write down the names."

As Erika Darago picked up the pen, Mackinnon felt his mobile vibrate in his jacket pocket. He fished it out. Tyler's name flashed on the screen.

Mackinnon looked back at the one-way mirror regretfully. As interesting as this was, he had work to do, and DI Tyler obviously wanted him to get back to the incident room.

"It's Tyler," Mackinnon said to Charlotte. "We better get back."

Mackinnon didn't answer the call. The viewing area wasn't completely soundproof. Instead he and Charlotte took the stairs two at a time, and found Tyler in the incident room, standing beside Collins's desk.

Mackinnon, Tyler and Charlotte were mulling over the possibility that Remi Darago was their Mr. X, when DCI Brookbank burst into the room.

He held up a sheet of white paper.

"We've got the list from Erika Darago," he said, but he didn't look jubilant or even vaguely pleased.

He looked nervous.

Mackinnon felt his chest tighten. What had happened?

"Francis Eze isn't on it, but we've got Adam Jonah and Mark Fleming."

There were celebratory shouts and slaps on the back around the incident room, but Mackinnon stayed still, staring at Brookbank.

He knew something else was coming.

Then Brookbank dropped his bombshell.

"The trouble is," Brookbank said. "There's a new name on the end of the list."

The incident room fell silent.

Brookbank paused, and he turned his head, making sure he had the attention of everyone in the room.

Mackinnon felt the weight of Brookbank's gaze.

"It's a woman. We need to find her fast."

CHAPTER THIRTY-TWO

ALFIE SAT IN A DOORWAY, opposite the block of flats, bundled up in his coat.

It was getting dark, but there was still a police car outside Manor Park House, which was good. That meant they were taking it seriously. Hopefully the police would take away his aunt and uncle for good and punish Mr. X for what he did to Francis.

It was getting cold now. Alfie tightened the coat around him, pulling the zipper up right to his chin, and buried the lower half of his face in the collar so the warmth of his breath warmed his body.

He'd bought a packet of custard creams for eighty pence, and a carton of chocolate milk from the corner shop, but he'd polished those off an hour ago. He really wanted something warm to eat, but he didn't have enough money left for chips.

He knew there must be police inside Manor Park House, but he hadn't seen the woman he'd spoken to earlier.

She'd told him her name was Charlotte, but he didn't know her last name. Alfie looked up at the block of flats, his aunt and uncle's flat was now dark. Maybe the police had finished in there, but then why was the squad car still outside?

Alfie was scared. If Charlotte had been there, he might have gone to her and told her everything, but the two officers Alfie had seen leaving the squad car were two big burly men who reminded him of Mr. Xander, and Alfie didn't want to talk to them.

He wasn't even sure if they'd found his uncle yet. Alfie had kept a close watch to see if his Uncle Remi had returned from work, but he hadn't seen him. He knew the police had Aunt Erika, but what if they didn't believe Uncle Remi was involved?

What if the police made him go home with Uncle Remi? Alfie shuddered.

He'd gone to see the Oracle, hoping the old man could help him get in touch with his grandmother, but the Oracle had been busy with a ritual, and Alfie didn't want to talk to him with all those people around. Still, he was glad he'd gone. If he hadn't, he would never have met Charlotte and his aunt would still have been at home.

Maybe he could ask the police if he could go and live with his grandmother again. If Alfie promised to be on his best behaviour and not get into any more trouble, she might take him back.

Alfie rummaged through the empty packet of biscuits,

scraping his finger along the plastic wrapper to collect the crumbs and then licking them off his fingers.

He needed someone he could trust. Someone who could help him.

He still didn't have any credit on his mobile phone, so he couldn't phone his grandmother. There had to be someone who could help him within walking distance.

Alfie thought about the female police officer, Charlotte, but he didn't even know which station the female officer worked at. She could be anywhere.

Alfie didn't have a choice. There was only one other person he could think of.

Alfie stood up and dusted the biscuit crumbs off the front of his coat. He picked up his empty carton of chocolate milk and stuffed the empty biscuit wrapper inside.

Carefully peering out to make sure that the police were still inside the building, and they weren't going to see him, Alfie came out of his little hiding place by the doorway and clambered down the steps.

He knew exactly where he was going. He walked the same route to school every morning.

He would go to Mr. Xander's house. He might be a bit strict, but Mr. Xander was a teacher. It was his job to look after kids.

Surely, he'd be able to help.

CHAPTER THIRTY-THREE

GERMAINE OKORO GOT UP STIFFLY from his armchair. He'd been sitting in the same position for hours, trying to decide on the best course of action.

He'd promised the police officer that as soon as he had any information about the identity of Mr. X, he'd be in touch.

But at the time he had no idea what he would find. He hadn't realised how damaging this could be to his family, and the wider community. The information was explosive, and it would send shockwaves through the congregation. That's why he couldn't act before he was absolutely certain he had all the facts.

Germaine Okoro tried to be a good man. Since the death of his wife, ten years ago, he'd brought Kwame up as a single parent. It hadn't been easy. He missed his wife every day.

He walked across to the mantelpiece and picked up a framed photograph of his wife.

"What should I do, Gloria?" he muttered.

The Oracle was supposed to be a leader. He was meant to be a guide to his followers, but who would help *him*?

He had performed a ritual, calling on the spirits for guidance, but for the first time in his life, they had failed him.

As an Oracle, he wasn't used to feeling so confused and lost. He was supposed to have confidence in his actions.

Normally, the spirits were there to guide him and show him the right path. But today they were silent. He had never felt so alone in his life.

He looked at the photograph of Gloria again. It didn't get any easier. He wished she was here, so they could talk things through.

He took a deep breath and asked himself: What would Gloria do?

And suddenly, he knew.

He ran a thumb over the silver picture frame and set it back down.

He knew exactly what he needed to do. It wouldn't be easy, but it was the right path.

He walked out into the hallway and stood beside the little telephone table. He opened the drawer of the telephone table and rummaged around until he found what he was looking for: the card he'd been given by DC Charlotte Brown of the City of London Police.

Germaine's hand shook slightly as he dialled.

The phone was answered by a male voice, who told him that DC Brown was otherwise engaged and asked him if he would like to leave a name and a message.

Germaine Okoro gazed at the ceiling. He could feel his confidence ebbing away. He needed to speak to somebody now, or his courage and conviction would fail completely.

"I really need to speak to someone," Germaine said. "It's quite urgent."

The man on the phone took down Germaine's details and asked him to hold for a moment. He said he was going to try and find someone Germaine could speak to.

For the longest ninety seconds of his life, Germaine stood in his hallway and listened to the static silence on the other end of the line.

Perhaps this was a sign from the spirits. Perhaps he shouldn't speak to the police?

Germaine's grip on the telephone slackened, and he was about to lower the receiver when a male voice spoke up.

"Mr. Okoro? This is DS Mackinnon. I understand you wanted to speak to Charlotte. I'm afraid she is occupied at the moment. Can I help?"

Germaine Okoro remembered Mackinnon. He was the tall police officer, who'd come to see him at the start of the investigation. Yes, Germaine thought, he would do.

"Yes," Germaine said. "I'd like to speak to you. It's a bit complicated to explain over the phone, but I think I know who this Mr. X is."

"Can you tell me now?"

Germaine could hear the urgency in Mackinnon's voice.

199

"The thing is," Germaine Okoro said. "It's very complicated, and I don't really have any proof."

There was a sharp clunk in the kitchen followed by a rustle.

Germaine Okoro frowned. What was that? There was nobody else in the house. Kwame was supposed to be at college.

He put a hand over the lower part of the receiver and took a step towards the kitchen, but he didn't hear anything else.

DS Mackinnon was talking at him down the phone, but Germaine was distracted by another rustle.

"I'm sorry," Germaine said. "I have to go now, but if you could come round soon, I'll be happy to tell you what I know."

The Oracle didn't wait for an answer and hung up the phone.

"Kwame?" he called. "Is that you?"

He put a hand on the kitchen door and gently eased it open.

The kitchen was empty. He took another step forward, shaking his head. He was getting jumpy, imagining things, but that was hardly surprising given the circumstances.

That's funny, Germaine thought. A red velvet pouch sat on the kitchen counter. How odd.

Germaine reached out to pick up the pouch, but before he could, he felt a hand grasp a handful of his hair, shoving his head backwards and exposing his throat.

Germaine Okoro saw the flash of a blade. He noticed the

handle—dark wood, with a notch in the side. It was the one he used for sacrificing chickens. It was a ritual knife.

Germaine Okoro knew what was coming next. He felt a warm rush of blood as the blade slashed its way across his neck.

The spirits have mercy, he thought, as he began to choke on his own blood.

CHAPTER THIRTY-FOUR

"FOR GOD'S SAKE," MACKINNON SAID as he heard the dial tone. "What was that all about? Why couldn't the Oracle have just said what he wanted to over the phone?"

He hung up the phone.

The entire incident room was manic. Everyone was focused on tracking down the woman on Erika Darago's list, Lisa Stratton.

"We've got an address." DC Webb held up a piece of paper and waggled it above his head.

DI Tyler strode over to Webb's desk, grabbing the piece of paper and quickly scanning it.

He nodded at the telephone on DC Webb's desk "Get an available unit there straight away. Whoever is closest."

Tyler turned and looked around the room until his eyes focused on Charlotte.

"DC Brown." He handed her the sheet of paper. "You go

there, too. Try to explain the situation without scaring her half to death and bring her back here," he said.

Then he turned to Mackinnon.

"Mackinnon I want you to— "

But Mackinnon interrupted him. "I've just taken a call, sir, from the Oracle, Germaine Okoro. He told me he thinks he knows the identity of Mr. X."

Tyler stopped mid-stride. "And?"

"He didn't quite get round to telling me who he thought it was before he hung up."

Tyler's cheeks flushed, and he shook his head in disbelief. "Is he playing games?"

Mackinnon shrugged. "I don't know. He was acting quite strangely, but I don't think we should ignore it. I could go round there now?"

Tyler sighed and looked around the busy incident room. Mackinnon knew he wanted all bodies focused on tracking down Lisa Stratton.

Tyler hesitated for a moment then nodded and said, "All right go and speak to him. But be as quick as you can."

Mackinnon grabbed his jacket and mobile phone and set off for Germaine Okoro's house in Poplar.

Mackinnon reached Germaine Okoro's address in record time.

He knocked on the door, but there was no answer.

He waited at least two minutes, and then he leaned over the railings so he could peer into the front room.

Mackinnon swore under his breath. It didn't look like

Germaine Okoro was home. There was no sign of anyone. The TV was off, although the lights were still on.

Surely Germaine hadn't decided to go out straight after dropping the bombshell that he knew the identity of Mr. X.

Mackinnon pulled out his mobile and dialled the number for Germaine Okoro. He could hear the phone ringing inside. On and on, it rang. No one picked up.

He leaned down and stuck his fingers inside the letterbox, pushing it open, and looked inside.

Nothing. No movement. No evidence anyone was at home.

Mackinnon let the letterbox close and straightened up. He could really do without this. He should be working with the team, tracking down Lisa Stratton.

He was considering leaving a note when he remembered Germaine Okoro's garden. Could he be out there and just not hear Mackinnon knocking on the door?

It was a bit late for gardening, but it was worth a try.

Germaine Okoro's house was part of a terraced row. Behind the houses, there was a square communal area with a small green. Mackinnon thought he might be able to access the back garden from there.

Mackinnon jogged around the back of the buildings, counting the number of houses so he knew that he had the right number. He knocked on the wooden fence separating the Oracle's garden from the green.

Still nothing.

It wasn't in Mackinnon's nature to give up easily. He needed to know what the Oracle knew about Mr. X.

He pushed the gate, but it stubbornly remained shut.

It gave a little at the bottom and not at the top, so Mackinnon guessed that's where the lock was. Standing close to the fence, he reached over, grasping at the other side, trying to locate the lock.

His fingers closed around a metal latch.

Pushing it down, he heard a click. Mackinnon smiled. Bingo.

He pushed open the gate. There was no sign in the small terraced garden of Germaine Okoro. The plants were still lush and green, some still flowering, like the brilliant scarlet fuchsias.

The Oracle wasn't here. Mackinnon couldn't believe it. After what he had said on the phone, surely Germaine Okoro would have been expecting a visit.

Mackinnon walked briskly down the garden path, which ran along the centre of the garden towards the house. He decided to knock on the back door just in case.

The back door was made from white uPVC and a glass panel, which covered the top third of the door. It led straight into the kitchen.

There was a set of French doors to his right, which led into the open plan lounge-diner. That was where he and Charlotte had entered the garden on their first visit to Germaine Okoro.

The light was on in the lounge and Mackinnon could see it was empty.

Mackinnon knocked, then put his face close to the window. His breath steamed the glass.

The lights were off in the kitchen, making it much harder to see inside.

As his eyes adjusted to the dim light, he saw something near the refrigerator.

On the white and black chequered floor, was the body of a man. Had Germaine Okoro fallen or collapsed? He wasn't a young man.

Mackinnon reached for the mobile with one hand, his other hand grabbed the door handle.

Someone must have heard his prayers because the kitchen door was unlocked.

He rushed into the kitchen and knelt down beside the Oracle.

An ugly red welt ran the length of the man's throat.

Surely no one could have survived that.

Mackinnon felt Okoro's blood seep into his trousers as he knelt on the floor.

He wasn't going to be able to stem the bleeding. He pulled out his mobile phone to call it in when he heard a movement behind him.

He turned sharply.

But he wasn't quick enough.

He didn't see anyone before the blow to his head had him reeling towards the floor.

The first blow made him see black and white spots.

He lay, dazed, over the body of Germaine Okoro. He had to move. Had to get help.

Mackinnon was trying to push himself upwards when the second blow caught him on the other side of the head.

This time he went down and didn't get up.

CHAPTER THIRTY-FIVE

MACKINNON WOKE UP WITH A blinding headache. The pain was so strong that, for a moment, he couldn't focus on anything else.

The pain seemed to reverberate around his head, in waves, clawing its way upwards from the base of his spine.

It was only when he tried to move his arms, he realised he'd been tied up.

He jerked and pulled, but the ties held fast. They were made of some kind of plastic. Maybe cable ties? The more he pulled, the more they cut into his wrists.

He was sitting on a chair. When he leaned forward, he could see that thick, blue plastic cable ties had been looped around his ankles and around the chair legs.

Mackinnon looked around the room. He was still in the Oracle's house.

Everything came flooding back. Whoever had hit him over the head had tied him up and left him here.

How long ago had he been knocked unconscious? How long had he been tied up?

He could still feel the wetness from the blood that had soaked into his trousers as he'd kneeled beside Germaine Okoro. The blood hadn't yet dried so he couldn't have been tied up for long.

He felt his mobile phone vibrating in his trouser pocket. Shit. There was no way in hell he could reach it.

As far as he could see, he had two options: try to free himself of the restraints or make enough noise that the neighbours realise there is something wrong and call the police.

But whoever hit him over the head could still be here.

Mackinnon might not have long before whoever it was came back. He needed to get free of these restraints.

Mackinnon jerked his arm upwards as hard as he could and tried to pull one arm out of the restraints, but it was no good. They weren't loosening.

He turned his attention to the ties around his ankles.

It was dark in the room and difficult to see, but he thought each tie had only been wrapped around the chair leg. All he had to do was try and lift the chair upwards slightly, and he should be able to slide his legs down, and at least free his ankles.

It wasn't as easy as he thought. The plastic ties were tight, and he managed to only ease them down a centimetre at a time.

Mackinnon was sweating.

He could hear the faint rumble of traffic from outside, but he couldn't hear anyone in the house.

He hadn't even managed to call for backup, before he'd been hit.

He wondered if Germaine Okoro's body was still lying on the kitchen floor. If the man hadn't been dead when Mackinnon found him, he would have bled out by now.

Mackinnon's mobile phone began to vibrate with an incoming call again.

Surely someone would realise there was a problem if they couldn't reach him.

Frustrated with how little progress he was making, Mackinnon tried to lift the chair and stagger over to the wall.

If the chair had been made of wood, he could have bashed it into the wall until it shattered but making so much noise would bring attention. If whoever had hit him was still here that was the last thing he needed.

As far as he could tell from the feel of the legs, and the way they glinted in the light coming in through the window from the street lights outside, they were metal.

Mackinnon looked around the room for anything else that could help him get free.

In the centre of the room, there was a large glass-topped table. It was probably shatterproof glass, but with enough force he could break it, and then use a sharp edge to try and wear down the plastic tying up his wrists.

But again, that would make too much noise, and it would take even longer than trying to shatter the chair.

It was no good. Mackinnon couldn't just sit there. He would have to try and break the chair and hope whoever had hit him was not still in the house.

Mackinnon leaned the chair forward on two legs. Leaning on the balls of his feet, he tried to straighten up as far as he could.

His wrists burned as the plastic bit into them.

Mackinnon turned the chair around and moved back towards the wall. He wanted to use an external wall. If he tried to use an internal one, chances were the legs would just go through the plasterboard.

He braced himself, and then tried to run backwards, pointing the chair outwards, so it took the full impact as he crashed into the wall.

The impact sent reverberations all along his spine. Mackinnon saw stars. He staggered a little, and then his ankle twisted, and he fell down to his knees.

It hadn't worked. The bloody chair legs were bent but not broken.

It was hard getting to his feet. He was really sweating now, and the chair had shifted behind him, making it impossible to straighten up or to move one leg without the other. So he had to try and jump to his feet, which took four attempts.

He lined up the run again, and this time, there was a sickening crash as he knocked into the wall. Two of the chair legs fell to the ground.

Mackinnon stood there, still bent over at the waist, waiting and listening. If there was someone else in the house they would definitely have heard that.

He tried to lean down and grab one of the chair legs. He couldn't move his arms much, so it wasn't a very effective weapon, but it was better than nothing.

Long moments passed in silence. There couldn't be anyone else here. They would have come to investigate.

He set himself up and rammed again. This time he felt the back of the chair start to give way. He was almost there.

Mackinnon pulled his arms back, feeling the burn between his shoulder blades, and managed to loop his arms over the top of the chair.

The rest of the chair clattered to the floor.

His hands were still tied behind his back, but his legs were now free. He kept a tight hold of the shattered metallic chair leg, which was just a hollow tube.

He stumbled towards the door, praying it wouldn't be locked.

Mackinnon depressed the handle and pushed, but the door didn't budge.

Mackinnon swore under his breath. He took a quick look at the door hinges.

Would it be easier to get them off somehow than to break it down?

He tapped it with a knuckle. It sounded pretty solid for an internal door.

He could kick the handle off, then hope that he could find something to manipulate the lock.

As he stood there sweating, considering his options, he heard a noise.

He took a step back from the door. The element of surprise would give him his best shot.

Mackinnon flattened his back against the wall. When they came in the room, he would be hidden for a split-second, giving him the advantage.

He could hear voices. More than one.

Mackinnon's chest tightened. He might have a chance if it was one man alone... But two? And with his hands tied behind his back?

He had no chance.

He felt a trickle of sweat crawl down his spine.

Then he heard something he really wasn't expecting.

"Mackinnon?"

He recognised that voice. Collins.

"In here." Mackinnon's voice sounded hoarse. He kicked the door.

He saw the door handle depress.

"It's locked," Collins said.

"I know," Mackinnon said. "Can you break it down?"

"You break it down," Collins said. "You're bigger than I am."

"It'll break easier from your side," Mackinnon said. "Come on put your back into it."

Mackinnon could hear Collins's muttered complaints from behind the door, then Collins said, "All right, stand back."

There was a dull thud against the door, but it stood firm.

"That's not going to work," Mackinnon said. "You need to do it harder."

"Thanks for the advice."

Two seconds later, the door exploded open, and Collins launched himself into the room, landing spreadeagled on the floor.

The door was hanging off its hinges. "Nice work," Mackinnon said.

Collins swore, cradling his shoulder. "Christ, that hurt. I think I've dislocated it," he said. "Help us up, would you?"

Mackinnon turned around so Collins could see that his hands were otherwise occupied.

"Germaine Okoro," Mackinnon said. "I found him in the kitchen. Is he—?"

"He's dead," Collins said. "You weren't answering your mobile, so Tyler asked me to check on you. I saw the back gate open. I've got a uniform unit with me. They are checking upstairs."

Mackinnon nodded, making a mental note to thank DI Tyler.

"Who did it? Who tied you up?" Collins asked.

Mackinnon shook his head. "No idea, I came to talk to the Oracle. There was no answer so I came around the back and saw him lying there with his throat cut. The door was open so I went to check on him. I reached for my phone to call for backup, but the next thing I knew, someone had hit me over the head, and then I woke up in here. Tied up to that." Mackinnon nodded at the broken chair on the floor.

Collins shook his head. "It's always you, isn't it?"

"What do you mean?"

"Always going off and getting into trouble."

"I wasn't looking for trouble. The Oracle said he had information about who Mr. X was."

Collins nodded. "I guess he didn't have time to tell you anything with his dying breath?"

Mackinnon shook his head. "I'm pretty sure he was dead when I got here. Any news on the girl, Lisa Stratton?"

"They're still trying to track her down. They've got her

address, but, unfortunately, she's not home. We contacted the financial company she works for, but she'd left for the day. Charlotte's at Lisa Stratton's flat now, talking to her flatmate."

"Well, I hope she's had more luck than me," Mackinnon said.

CHAPTER THIRTY-SIX

CHARLOTTE SHOVED HER HANDS IN her pockets and stared at the girl in front of her.

Kristen Deaver was Lisa Stratton's flatmate and right now, Charlotte believed she was the most annoying girl she had ever met.

When Charlotte had arrived at Lisa Stratton's flat, a uniformed unit was already there. They introduced themselves as PC Davies and PC Bell.

"She's not here," PC Bell, a tall, balding officer with a hooked nose, had said as soon as Charlotte had arrived.

"Well, where the hell is she?" Charlotte had said.

So far, she hadn't managed to get an answer.

Twenty-three year old Kristen Deaver was sitting on the beige sofa. She'd curled her legs under her, and she wore a pair of oversized, fluffy bunny rabbit slippers.

Kristen had given the uniformed officers Lisa Stratton's mobile number, but they hadn't been able to get through. It kept going straight through to her voicemail. According to Kristen, Lisa often let the battery go flat.

"Kristen," Charlotte said, "you must have some idea where Lisa is. This is really important. You're her flatmate. You must know what sort of places she goes to. Where does she usually go after work? The gym? For a drink?"

Kristen shrugged. "We're not really friends. We just share the flat. London is really expensive. I can't afford it on my own."

Just answer the bloody question, Charlotte thought. *I don't care about your finances.*

"Okay," Charlotte said slowly, trying to control her temper. "But she must mention some of the places she hangs out? You must know something about her life that could help."

Kristen scratched the corner of her nose. "Um, well she does go for a drink after work sometimes."

Finally. They were getting somewhere.

Charlotte leaned towards Kristen. "Where? Where does she go?"

"There are a couple of places," Kristen said, screwing up her face as if thinking hurt her brain.

"But usually she goes to the Walrus and the Carpenter because it's close to where she works."

"Right," Charlotte said, turning away and scrolling through her mobile phone. "We'll try there."

Kristen got to her feet. "Oh, that's good then. Are we done? Because I really need to get ready to go out. I've got a date tonight."

Charlotte raised a hand and clamped it to her ear, to block out Kristen's whiny voice.

"No," she snapped, "you're not going anywhere yet. Not until we've found Lisa Stratton."

Kristen huffed out a breath and flopped down on the sofa, shooting Charlotte a sulky look.

PC Davies and PC Bell were still milling about in the room talking.

Charlotte put a finger in her ear. The noise on the other end of the line was deafening. She could hear the sounds of revellers in the pub.

"This is DC Brown of the City of London police. I'm looking for Lisa Stratton. It's very urgent. Could you put a call out and see if she's there?"

Charlotte had to repeat herself another three times before the barman on the other end of the line understood what she was saying.

She listened with her heart in her mouth as she heard the barman shout out Lisa Stratton's name.

It seemed an eternity before the barman came back on the line and said, "Yeah she's here. Do you want to speak to her?"

"She's there. We've found her," Charlotte said, to PC Bell and PC Davies. "She's at the Walrus and Carpenter Pub, Monument Street."

PC Bell nodded. "Right. I know it. We'll call it in and head there now."

Charlotte nodded then turned her attention back to the phone. "Yes, please. I need to speak to her."

Charlotte paced the room while she waited for Lisa Stratton to come on the line. Why was it taking so long?

Then Charlotte heard a girly tinkle of laughter and a female voice said, "Hello?"

"Is this Lisa Stratton?" Charlotte asked.

"Um, yeah," Lisa Stratton said.

"Listen to me. This is very important. My name is DC Charlotte Brown of the City of London Police. I need to come and speak to you. You're not in any trouble, but it's imperative you stay where you are until we get there. Don't leave the bar. There will be uniformed officers there very shortly. Stay in the bar and wait for us, do you understand?"

There was a pause on the other end of the line, then Lisa Stratton said, "What is this all about? I haven't done anything wrong."

"No, you haven't done anything, but it's really important that we speak to you, do you understand?"

"Sorry, the line's not very good," Lisa said. "It's really noisy in here. Um, so maybe you could give me a ring tomorrow?"

"No," Charlotte said. "Wait, stay on the line. I need you to stay on the line."

"Yeah, sorry but I can hardly hear you," Lisa Stratton said. "You're kind of breaking up. Sorry," she said.

There was a scraping sound on the other end of the line.

"Hello," Charlotte said. "Lisa? Lisa, are you still there?"

The only response was the muffled sound of people laughing and talking, and the clinking of glasses.

What the hell was the girl playing at?

Charlotte eyed the stupid fluffy, bunny rabbit slippers Kristen was wearing as the woman poked out her lower lip in another sulk.

Charlotte imagined herself picking up one of the slippers and hitting the girl around the head with it. Why was everybody being so stupid today?

"Lisa, are you still there?" Charlotte shouted into the telephone.

But there was no response until finally Charlotte heard a click, and then silence.

She'd hung up on her. "Dammit."

Charlotte left the flat in a hurry, taking the stairs two at a time, and pressed redial on her mobile phone. It rang and rang, but this time the bar staff weren't answering.

This was ridiculous. What the hell was Lisa Stratton playing at?

CHAPTER THIRTY-SEVEN

LISA STRATTON HANDED BACK THE phone to the barman.

"Nuisance caller," she told him.

The barman shrugged and put the phone back on the hook.

As Lisa reached for her vodka and orange, her hand trembled a little.

"Who was that?" asked Matt Clarke, who was standing beside her.

"Oh, no one," she said. "It's not important."

Lisa had been having a great time before the phone call. She'd had a bit of a thing for Matt Clarke for months now, ever since their encounter at their company's Christmas party, but he hadn't made his move yet.

Tonight it was just the two of them rather than the usual crowd from work, and Lisa thought this might be the night that Matt finally made his move.

But he wouldn't be impressed if the police turned up looking for her.

She put her drink back down on the bar. What on earth could they want with her? She hadn't done anything wrong. Maybe it was a mistake. Maybe they were looking for another Lisa Stratton. It wasn't exactly an uncommon name.

But there had been something about the urgency of the police officer's voice on the phone that scared her.

She fought the urge to down her drink and leave the bar, pretending it had never happened. But she wasn't that stupid. She wouldn't just walk off. What if she was in some kind of danger?

She shot an anxious look around the bar. No one seemed to be paying her any attention. They were all concentrating on their drinks, focused on getting a little tipsy after work.

She directed a sideways glance at Matt, and then wished she hadn't. He was staring at her with a puzzled frown.

A horrible thought occurred to Lisa. How much did she really know about Matt? Was he some kind of weirdo the police were tracking?

She took a large gulp of her drink and felt the vodka burn the back of her throat.

"Do you want to go on somewhere?" Matt asked with a grin.

She used to find that grin attractive. She had liked his deep dimples and his shiny white teeth, but today his smile looked slightly sinister.

Lisa shook her head. "Er, no. I think I'm gonna stay here, thanks."

Matt shrugged. "Suit yourself," he said and waved to get the barman's attention.

Lisa glanced at the clock on the wall above the bar.

How long would the police take to get here, she wondered.

If it was as urgent as the policewoman said, they should be here soon.

Lisa turned away from the bar and looked out of the huge windows that lined the front of the pub.

Maybe she should wait outside. She didn't much fancy being escorted out of her local by uniformed officers.

But the detective had told her to wait inside the bar, and she would be safer inside. There were so many people around. Surely nothing could happen to her here.

She only had to wait a little longer. The police would be here soon…

Lisa gasped. *Oh, God.*

She remembered what she had in the inner zipped pocket of her handbag: a little something for later, to help her unwind.

It wasn't like she was a drug addict. She just liked to smoke a bit of weed in the evenings to relax. It helped her sleep.

She didn't have much on her, but what if they wanted to take her to the police station? What if they searched her bag?

Shit. Shit. Shit. She'd have to get rid of it somehow before they got here.

She put one hand in her bag, unzipped the internal

pocket, and her fingers closed around the cling film-encased weed.

She groaned.

"I'm just going to the ladies'," she said to Matt and slipped down off the stool.

She needn't have worried about Matt. He'd turned his amorous attentions to the blonde barmaid and had forgotten all about Lisa.

Bastard.

As she walked across the bar, her eyes scanned all the faces, trying to see if there was anyone that stood out.

She weaved her way through the crowds. It was absolutely packed tonight. It was always busy, but tonight they were all packed in like sardines.

She jumped as a large group of men in front of her exploded with laughter.

She stood still for a moment, calming herself, then carried on edging her way to the ladies' toilets.

A woman held the door open for her at the ladies' toilet. Lisa smiled at her and went in.

Inside, she rested her handbag on the edge of one of the sinks and rifled around until she found the small amount of weed bound in plastic wrap.

Lisa exhaled. Thank God.

She chucked it into one of the toilet bowls and flushed the chain.

As she walked out of the cubicle, she dusted her hands together, set her shoulders and took a step forward.

She faltered. There was a man in the ladies' toilets.

His dark skin looked shiny under the harsh glare of the

lights. His hair was cropped close to his head, and lines had been shaved into patterns on each side of his head.

Lisa took a step back. Oh, God. Why had she come in here alone?

Keep calm. It's okay. It was a mistake. He'd probably just had a few drinks and picked the wrong door.

Any second now he would realise his error and apologise and leave.

But he didn't.

He smiled at her lazily.

"Hello Lisa," he said. "I've been looking for you."

CHAPTER THIRTY-EIGHT

BY THE TIME CHARLOTTE GOT to the Walrus and the Carpenter Pub on Monument Street, the uniformed officers were already there.

She recognised PC Davies from Lisa Stratton's flat, he nodded in recognition and began to walk over.

Charlotte stayed at the main entrance, her eyes scanning the sea of faces. There were so many people in here. The place was rammed. That wasn't going to make it any easier to locate Lisa Stratton.

PC Davies reached her side. "She's not here," he said.

"What? How is that possible? I spoke to her. I told her to stay where she was until we got here.

"Well, she *was* here, but she isn't anymore. I've just spoken to a couple of the bar staff and a friend of hers called Matt Clarke." PC Davies nodded in the general direction of the bar. "About ten minutes ago, she went to the ladies' and didn't come back, according to her friend."

Charlotte's stomach was in knots. How could this have happened? She'd spoken to her on the phone. They'd been so close. How could she have slipped through their fingers?

Charlotte fumbled in her pocket for her phone.

"Are you sure?" she asked PC Davies. "You've checked every inch of this place?"

PC Davies nodded. "Yes, every inch. We even went into the ladies'."

Charlotte nodded. "Okay, so we need to find out where she went and if she was with someone. We need access to the CCTV."

PC Davies nodded. "We're already on it."

His radio crackled into life, and Charlotte moved past him as he answered it, heading towards the back of the pub.

Lisa Stratton might not be in the ladies' toilets any longer, but there might be something in there that held a clue to Lisa's whereabouts.

Charlotte entered the toilets. There was a woman standing by the sink applying a thick layer of lip gloss.

It wasn't Lisa Stratton. Charlotte moved forwards, pushing open all the cubicle doors in turn.

There was only one occupied. She rapped on it.

"Lisa Stratton?"

"No," an angry voice replied from inside the cubicle.

Charlotte waited anyway just to make sure. She pulled out a recent photograph of Lisa Stratton. Kristen Deaver had said she could take it from the flat.

Lisa smiled in the picture. Her chestnut-coloured hair shone and hung in waves around her face. Charlotte hoped, wherever Lisa was, she was still smiling.

A moment later, a short girl with frizzy red hair stepped out of the cubicle and shot Charlotte an angry look.

"There are other toilets free, you know," she said, gesturing to the empty cubicles.

Charlotte ignored her and took a last look at Lisa Stratton's photo. She'd have to call DI Tyler and let him know they'd lost her.

As Charlotte turned to leave the toilets, another woman entered. The woman walked into the first cubicle and then made a disgusted noise and walked out again.

She caught Charlotte's eye. "Some people are rank. Honestly, the things people leave in toilets."

The woman went into the next cubicle along, and Charlotte headed back to see what she was talking about.

She peered down into the white bowl and saw a green substance wrapped in plastic, floating in the water.

It looked like weed.

Was that Lisa's? Was that why she'd gone to the ladies' toilets rather than remaining in the bar?

This was one hell of a mess.

Charlotte left the toilets and headed over to PC Bell and PC Davies, who were talking to the bar manager.

"We're getting the CCTV from in here," PC Davies said. "Shouldn't take long."

Charlotte nodded and headed towards the exit. She was more interested in the CCTV from outside.

She pulled her mobile from her pocket and dialled.

DI Tyler answered on the second ring.

"News?" he snapped.

"She's not here, boss," Charlotte said. "We don't know where she's gone. Have you got anything on CCTV?"

"We're working on it. I'll give you a call back," Tyler said and hung up.

Outside of the pub there were more people gathered on the pavement, spilling over from inside.

Charlotte looked around at the area immediately surrounding the pub. There were three possible directions Lisa could have taken.

Which one would Lisa have chosen?

To Charlotte's right there was a pedestrian zone blocked off to traffic by bollards. Straight in front of her and to her left were two busy roads, jammed with a mass of rush hour traffic.

She could have taken a bus or hailed a cab… She could be anywhere by now.

Charlotte groaned. Their only chance was if she'd been picked up on CCTV. It was a busy area so chances were good one of the cameras would have picked her up.

Charlotte's phone rang and she snatched it up. "DC Brown," she said.

It was Tyler.

"We've got a visual from eight minutes ago. Lisa Stratton with a tall, young, black male on Pudding Lane. It doesn't look good."

Charlotte took a breath. "What do you mean it doesn't look good?"

"It looks like he's got a concealed weapon," Tyler said. "We are calling in SO19."

CHAPTER THIRTY-NINE

LISA STRATTON WHIMPERED AS SHE felt the man digging something cold and metallic into her back. She couldn't tell what it was, but she knew it wasn't good.

It had to be a knife or a gun.

Why her? What had she done? She didn't understand.

She stumbled a little in her heels, and the man jolted her violently.

"No funny business," he said. "Or I'll cut you here in the street."

Lisa bit down on her lip to stop herself from crying. This couldn't be happening. It couldn't be real. There were so many people around.

How could a man be holding a weapon to her back like this without anyone realising anything was wrong?

"An interesting choice of pub, Lisa," the man said.

He stood so close to her she could feel his breath on her cheek. She shuddered.

"The Walrus and the Carpenter. It's from a poem by Lewis Carroll, are you a fan?"

Lisa Stratton shook her head. She went to the pub because it was the closest one to work. Although if she ever got out of this alive, there was no way she was going back.

He turned right, guiding her through some bollards into a pedestrianised area of the road. Someone had tied a bicycle to one of the bollards, and Lisa caught the corner of her ankle on the pedal as they walked past. She gasped.

"I'm warning you," he said. "I don't care who's around. I promise you, I'll do it, and I'll enjoy it."

"I'm sorry, it was the bike," Lisa said.

"Shut up," he said. "I didn't give you permission to talk."

This part of the road was quieter than the rest, despite the fact it was rush hour.

There should have been hundreds of people finishing work and pouring out the office buildings, but as they turned to walk towards the Monument, the number of people lessened.

She bit her bottom lip so hard she tasted blood. She was in central London. How could something like this go un-noticed?

"Pretty isn't it?" the man asked, nodding at the Monument.

"Do you know what it's for?" he asked.

She couldn't believe this. He had a weapon wedged against her ribs, and now he wanted to talk about London history.

She stayed silent.

"You should pay more attention to the city you work in Lisa," he said, patronisingly. "It's to commemorate the Great Fire of London. Do you see how tall it is? The column's height marks the distance to the site of the bakery in Pudding Lane where the fire started."

She ignored him. Freaky, weirdo creep.

Lisa knew where she was. The street would open out again soon. There would be more people around, and she could make a dash for it.

She went to walk ahead, but he pulled her sharply right into Pudding Lane. Her right shoe caught on the side of the pavement.

"Stop dragging your heels," he said. "I'm warning you. If you behave yourself, you'll get out of this unhurt, but if you mess me about..." he left the rest of the sentence unsaid, but Lisa focused on what he *had* said.

He would let her go if she did everything he asked. He'd set her free.

He turned again, and to Lisa's surprise, he headed for the stairs down to Monument Underground Station.

Where the hell was he taking her?

She reached out for the handrail to steady herself as they descended. He had one hand resting on her shoulder, and his other hand kept the weapon pressed into her side.

People were pouring out of the station. It seemed like hundreds of them were walking past, and not one of them paid a blind bit of notice. Lisa wanted to scream.

But he said if she behaved he'd let her go. She couldn't risk it.

They stood downstairs on the platform waiting for the

District line. It was packed, but they only had to wait for thirty seconds before the train rumbled in.

"This one," he said, nudging her forward.

Lisa stumbled ahead, stepping onto the train. The lights felt hot and brighter down here.

The seats were all full, and five people stood by the sliding doors.

Lisa found herself wedged between the glass separating the seats from the standing positions and the man who was holding the weapon to her back.

He leaned forward to whisper in her ear.

"Act natural," he said in a sing-song voice.

Lisa looked at the other passengers in the carriage. They all stared blankly ahead. She tried to catch someone's eye, but she knew it was hopeless. People always ignored each other on the tube.

What if he was lying?

What if he wasn't going to let her go? This could be her only chance.

There was a small Asian woman sitting in the seat closest to them. She had the handle of a carrier bag wrapped round her wrist, and she was bundled up in a thick coat and scarf. Lisa glanced down at the woman's feet. She was wearing sensible shoes, and she was staring across the aisle at her reflection in the glass.

Lisa held her breath and moved her foot forward, nudging the woman, staring at her, willing her to notice.

At first the woman didn't respond, and on the third nudge, she looked up sharply and gave Lisa a spiteful look, before shuffling her feet out of the way, out of Lisa's reach, and returning her gaze to the window.

No! Why was nobody paying any attention?

She wanted to cry. But at least the man behind her hadn't noticed.

She glanced over her shoulder at him, and he gave her a long lazy smile.

"Not far to go now," he said.

Lisa gazed wildly around the carriage. There were men in here. At least ten tall, strong men. Surely they could overpower the man behind her. If she could just make a dash for it…

She focused on the man closest to her. A businessman, wearing a grey suit. His face was almost as grey as his suit under the underground lights. He seemed to blend all into one. He held a paper in front of him, folded into a tiny square, as he scratched some letters onto it.

Jesus, Lisa thought, I am being held hostage by a madman just two feet away, and he's doing the bloody crossword.

She looked further down the carriage at a young woman with a toddler sitting on her knee. The woman was oblivious to Lisa, but the little boy in his red jacket and wellington boots stared up at her.

He noticed. The little boy realised something was wrong. Lisa tried to wave at him, but it didn't have the effect she'd hoped for. The boy pulled a face, as if he might cry, and turned back towards his mother.

The train was slowing for a stop. She pressed as close to

the piece of glass as she could, moving out of the way of the passengers disembarking.

She could run now while the door was open and make a dash for it. If she timed it just right, the doors might close on him and he might get stuck or at least delayed.

But she hesitated too long. More passengers had climbed aboard, and then there was a beep and the doors closed.

It's okay, Lisa told herself. She'd do it at the next station. The next stop would be where she made her move.

It was silly to try and get away when she was trapped inside the same carriage. Her only chance would be to do it as they got off the train.

She didn't believe him when he said he'd let her go. She'd be stupid to trust him.

She had to try and make a break for it herself.

CHAPTER FORTY

MACKINNON WALKED UP THE STAIRS at Wood Street Station, rubbing his sore wrists. He was grateful he'd got back in one piece, but his head was killing him.

"You need to get yourself checked out," Collins said. "You're going to have a lump the size of an egg on the side of your head."

On instinct, Mackinnon reached up and touched his temple, then winced. Collins was right.

"Yeah. I might go after work tonight," Mackinnon said.

As soon as they entered the incident room, DC Webb called them over.

"We've got the girl on CCTV."

Mackinnon and Collins hurried over to Webb's desk.

DC Webb angled his monitor so they could see the images on the screen.

"We've got some screenshots of Lisa Stratton with an

IC3 male leaving the Walrus and Carpenter Pub." Webb pointed a finger at the screen.

Mackinnon swallowed and leaned closer to the monitor. He felt sick.

"That's Kwame," Mackinnon said. "Kwame Okoro, the Oracle's son."

DC Webb picked up the phone on his desk. "I'll tell Tyler."

The next few minutes passed in a blur.

They had CCTV footage of Lisa Stratton and Kwame Okoro leaving the underground station at Mile End, and then heading towards St Paul's Way, but they'd lost them after Kwame took a left turn into the Towers Estate.

DI Tyler stood at the front of the room. His tie was askew and his face looked almost as creased as his shirt.

"Listen up," he said. "DC Webb has got the latest update."

He nodded to DC Webb who got up from his desk and walked towards the whiteboard and a map of East London and the City that was pinned to the green board next to it.

A blue line snaked along the map from Monument Street to the Towers Estate.

"This is the route they've taken," DC Webb said, pointing to the blue line.

"We've lost him on the CCTV, but we know they entered the Towers Estate. Which means they are somewhere in this area."

DC Webb drew a circular shape with a red marker pen, highlighting the Towers Estate.

"He must still be in there. If he'd come out we would have seen him."

Tyler nodded. "It's not a very big area. We've got uniform going door-to-door at the moment. SO19 are on standby, but we don't believe Kwame Okoro has a gun. On a section of the CCTV footage, Okoro's coat slipped back a little and gave us a better view of the weapon. It looks like a knife."

That was something at least, but Mackinnon didn't think Lisa Stratton would find it that reassuring.

"We need to keep monitoring all CCTV cameras in the area. We also need to look into Kwame Okoro's background. Does he have friends or family in the Towers Estate? We need to find out where he is heading."

Tyler frowned and gazed around the room. "I don't need to remind you that we are dealing with a very dangerous man. He is our prime suspect for the murders of Francis Eze, Adam Jonah, Mark Fleming and his own father, Germaine Okoro. And now he has Lisa Stratton. He has a hostage.

"We need to act fast, but methodically. We can't miss anything."

The impromptu briefing ended fast. Officers, analysts and admin staff rushed to get back to their desks. Everyone worked with the same sense of urgency.

Just a few moments later, Evie Charlesworth stood up. Her cheeks were flushed, and she was clutching a printout.

"We've got him," she said. "He used his credit card to order a delivery to an address in the Towers Estate four days ago. Forty-two, Victoria House."

Tyler reached for the printout and quickly scanned the contents as he reached for the phone on Evie's desk.

Tyler barked a few instructions down the phone.

After he hung up, he started to dial again, then looked up.

"We've got a squad car in the vicinity," DI Tyler said. "They're on their way there now. I want you and you…" He jabbed his thumb at Collins and Mackinnon. "…to get over there, too. I need to fill in DCI Brookbank."

This time Collins and Mackinnon didn't bother with public transport. Collins checked out a squad car. They pulled out into the city traffic with the sirens blaring.

Collins had taken the advance driving course, but Mackinnon still grabbed the edges of the passenger seat as Collins weaved the car in and out of the rush hour traffic.

"Come on!" Collins slapped his hand on the dashboard. "They can see the sodding lights and hear the sirens, but what do they do? They move about five inches. Tell me, how am I meant to get through that gap?"

Mackinnon didn't answer. He was busy scrolling through his phone, checking for updates.

Mackinnon glanced at the clock. It had only been half an hour since Lisa Stratton had been seen on CCTV, but Kwame Okoro could have done a lot of damage in thirty minutes.

Mackinnon hoped they weren't too late.

CHAPTER FORTY-ONE

LISA STRATTON SOBBED AS SHE rested her forehead against the wooden floorboards. How could this be happening to her? It couldn't be real. It had to be a dream. A nightmare.

He'd tied her up.

Her wrists were bound with blue cable ties and looped around a metal stake buried in the floorboards. Her legs were tied together too, and he had his knee pressing down onto the small of her back, so she was pinned to the ground.

Lisa could hardly move. She sobbed again.

"Shut up," he said.

She could hear him sharpening the blade. The sound of the knife sliding against stone sent shivers up Lisa's back, and she sobbed again.

She couldn't help it.

She should have run as soon as they'd surfaced from the

underground station, but it all happened so fast, and then all of a sudden they were in an alleyway, and there was no one else around.

What could she have done? He'd promised to let her go, if she behaved. And she had. She had done everything he'd asked.

"You said you'd let me go," she sniffed. "You promised."

"Hmm." The man chuckled. "Did I really?"

"Yes," she sniffed.

Her forehead rubbed against the dirty bare floorboards. "You said if I did everything you wanted, you'd let me go. Please. Why are you doing this? I haven't done anything to you," she said.

"You're not thinking straight," the man said, as he sharpened his knife again. "It's not what you've done to me. It's what you've done to someone else."

Someone else? Lisa arched her back, trying to turn and face him, but it was no good. His knee had firmly pinned her to the floor.

"What do you mean? I haven't done anything to anybody."

"Well, that can't be true, Lisa."

The man shifted his position slightly, so he could see her face.

"Look, it's nothing personal," he said, and he moved a lock of her hair, tucking it behind her ear almost tenderly.

"Someone paid me to do this, Lisa. Can you guess who it was?"

Someone paid him? The thought rolled around in Lisa's

head, but it didn't make any sense. Who the hell would want someone to do this to her?

"I tell you what, I'm a fair man," he said. "If you guess correctly, I'll let you go."

"Really?" Lisa said.

She raised her head, suddenly alert, racking her brains to come up with someone she'd annoyed or someone she'd hurt.

Six months ago, she'd broken up with Robert, but that had been a mutual thing. It couldn't have been him. Maybe someone at work? There had been a data inputter at work who'd expected a promotion, and when it was given to Lisa, she'd been very annoyed... But surely she wouldn't have gone this far. Not over something as stupid as a promotion.

"Tick tock," the man said. "Time's running out."

"No," Lisa said, desperately. "Wait! I just need to think. I can't concentrate when you're sharpening that knife."

"Well, you don't really have any choice," he said. "Although, I think it might be sharp enough now. What do you think?"

He shoved the blade close to her face, and she recoiled, trying to move backwards, but she couldn't move. He had her wedged against the floor.

Tears trickled out from the corners of her eyes, making the floor wet beneath her cheek.

"Wait!"

Lisa remembered something. But it had been more than a year ago, surely that couldn't be it...

And it wasn't as if Lisa was to blame. He had deserved it.

"Oh dear, time is up," the man said in that horrible sing-song voice of his.

"No wait," Lisa said. "I know who it is."

The man set down the knife. She heard it clunk against the floorboards as it came to rest beside her head.

"Really?" the man asked. "Who do you think it is?"

"I think it's Bertie, Bertie Lassiter."

The man chuckled, and Lisa knew she was right.

That bastard. Bertie had been a real creep. He'd been high up in the firm Lisa worked for, and he'd thought it was his God-given right to squeeze the backsides of all the women who worked there. He didn't even try to be discrete about it, either.

But he'd made a mistake when he'd gone a step too far with Lisa.

He'd trapped her in one of the stationery cupboards and tried to put his hand up her skirt.

Well, the other girls might have taken the harassment, but not Lisa. She'd gone straight to HR and threatened to take legal action.

It had caused a right stink. The girls Bertie had harassed were on her side, of course, all the women in the office were, but the men thought she'd just taken Bertie's 'friendli-ness' the wrong way. But Lisa stuck to her guns. The management had to do something, or she would take legal action.

Bertie had been furious.

The company wanted to hush up the incident. Bertie might not have been charged with anything, but he lost his job and with whispers in the city being like they were, as far as Lisa knew, he hadn't got another one.

"I'm right, aren't I?" she asked him. "It's Bertie. You said you'd let me go now. Please let me go."

Lisa started to struggle against her restraints.

The man laughed, and it gave Lisa a hollow feeling in the pit of her stomach.

"I was only joking," he said. "Don't be silly. Why would I let you go? The five grand will go a long way to pay off my student loans, you know. No offence. It is just money to me," he said.

"Five grand," Lisa repeated.

Five measly grand. Was that all her life was worth?

She struggled wildly. "I'll pay you more than that. I've got money," she said. "I've got ten grand in my bank account. Please. I'll pay you. I promise."

"Tempting as that offer is," he said. "I'll have to turn you down I'm afraid. It wouldn't be very sensible. As soon as I let you go, you'd go straight to the police, and then I'd be locked up with no money. As you can imagine, that's not a scenario I'm keen on."

She heard a scrape against the floorboards as he picked up the knife.

"Oh, God, no. Please. I won't go to the police. I promise. Please."

Lisa screamed, and he smacked her head roughly against the floor.

"Stop that," he said. "It won't make it any easier."

He shoved a rag into her mouth.

Between her sobs and the rag blocking off most of her air supply, she was starting to feel light-headed. That was probably a good thing.

She gazed at the wall and she saw the man's shadow.

He slowly raised the knife, muttering some words Lisa didn't understand.

Lisa felt strangely detached from her body.

He wrenched the top of her blouse and she heard the fabric rip as he slashed it with the blade.

Lisa couldn't get enough air. She was panting.

She shuddered as the cold metallic blade slipped beneath the back of her bra and felt a ping as he cut through the elastic.

Lisa's whole body was racked with sobs.

"Sorry about that," he said. "I need to leave a little mark here. It's my calling card."

And with a finger, he trailed a line diagonally from her left shoulder blade to her right hip and then from her right shoulder blade to her left hip.

"It'll only hurt for a moment," he said.

Lisa screamed, but it was muffled by the rag in her mouth.

She'd never been religious, but right now, she prayed to every God she could think of.

Lisa thought it wasn't possible to be more scared than she was now, but when the knife pierced the skin on her shoulder, and she felt the sharp cold sting, she screamed and screamed.

As he pulled the knife downwards, the pain grew more intense, until the shock and the pain overwhelmed her and everything faded to black.

She didn't even hear the commotion at the door.

CHAPTER FORTY-TWO

WHEN MACKINNON AND COLLINS ARRIVED at Victoria House, the road leading to the tower block was blocked off by squad cars.

There were four officers hastily erecting cordons on the street outside Victoria House. Mackinnon suspected that more uniformed officers had been stationed at the back of the block of flats to prevent other residents of the Towers Estate getting too close.

They showed their ID, and one of the officers waved the car through.

Collins parked up behind a squad car some distance away from the mayhem.

As they got out of the car, Mackinnon looked around. Who was in charge here? Had the building been evacuated yet?

He saw a group of officers a short distance away, grouped together, having an intense discussion. Mackinnon began to walk towards them. They were discussing a standoff situation. Kwame had barricaded himself in the flat with Lisa Stratton.

There was a shout.

Mackinnon and every other officer in the vicinity turned in the direction of the noise. A uniformed PC stood in the shadow of Victoria House, pointing upwards to the fourth floor.

Mackinnon looked up and saw Kwame Okoro, gripping an oversize knife standing on the balcony.

Kwame looped one leg over the black railing, and then lifted himself over. He stood perilously close to the edge of the balcony.

Was he going to jump? Mackinnon remembered how only a few short months ago he'd been standing on the ledge of a second floor window, trying to escape poison gas. He had plummeted to the ground and ended up in hospital. Just looking at Kwame Okoro balanced on the edge of the balcony made him break out in a sweat.

An officer with a loudspeaker called out, telling Kwame not to resist arrest and commanding him to hand himself in.

"I don't think so," Kwame shouted to the officer.

Mackinnon held his breath as a burly officer appeared behind Kwame on the balcony. He made a grab for him. But Kwame Okoro was too quick. Then everything seemed to happen in slow motion as Kwame leapt from the balcony.

Kwame somehow managed to grab the railings of the balcony of the flat below and swung there for a moment, before dropping again to the next balcony.

He was almost at ground level.

But he couldn't get away. He was surrounded.

Kwame swung again, and this time he landed on the ground. The jolt from landing, pulled him off balance, so although he'd landed on his feet, he quickly fell back and landed on his backside.

Immediately, two officers were on top of him.

But he slashed his knife only inches away from their faces.

One of the officers aimed a Taser, but somehow Kwame moved out of reach.

"Looks as if the spirits are looking after me," Kwame yelled. "My father was wrong. I would have made a perfect Oracle."

And then he was running. Mackinnon didn't think he'd ever seen anyone run so fast.

"Shit," Mackinnon said.

"It's all right one of the officers said. We've got all the exits to the estate blocked off now. He can't get away."

But Mackinnon was worried. The Towers Estate had a network of interlinking alleyways, and if the residents saw a boatload of officers charging after a lone black male, no doubt someone would call it police brutality.

If some naive resident took pity on Kwame and hid him from the police, that would mean a door-to-door manhunt.

If they weren't careful, they could have a riot on their hands.

Brian Taylor looked in his rearview mirror, studying the teenager in the back of his cab.

He'd known it had been a mistake to pick him up. Why hadn't he trusted his instinct?

He knew why. His daughter's wedding was fast approaching, and the costs were escalating at an atrocious rate. He couldn't afford to turn down a fare.

The kid looked nervous. He didn't sit back in the seat like a normal passenger. Instead he perched on the edge, leaning forward.

He was going to do a runner, Brian thought. No doubt about it.

Brian had his first clue from the clothes the kid was wearing. Baggy jeans falling off his arse, and one of those ridiculous baseball caps. Brian had been asking for trouble picking him up.

And if the kid's clothes weren't enough, he'd asked to be taken to the Towers Estate. That had bells ringing loudly.

The taxi doors were locked, to stop runaways, but that didn't mean anything if the kid pulled a knife.

Those baggy jeans could be hiding anything.

"We're nearly there," Brian said to the boy. "It's going to be about fifteen quid."

The boy nodded, but made no effort to pull out his wallet and get the money ready.

Yep, definitely a runaway fare.

Brian would report him of course, but they hardly ever got caught.

Brian turned the cab into the Towers Estate and had to make an abrupt stop. A couple of uniformed officers stood in the road, controlling traffic.

Brian wound down his window. "What's the problem, officer?"

The tallest officer approached the cab. He paid more attention to the kid in the back than to Brian.

"No problem, sir. Carry on," he said eventually and waved Brian on.

Brian drove further into the Towers Estate. He didn't like coming here. Rain or shine, it always seemed gloomy. That was probably to do with the monstrous tower blocks blocking out the sun.

"You can stop here," the teenager said.

Brian pulled over to the curb.

"Fifteen pounds, please," Brian said, looking at the boy in his rearview mirror.

When the kid pulled out a switchblade instead of cash, Brian only felt a frisson of fear for a moment. His overwhelming emotion was anger. The little fucker. Going through life on the take and screwing over honest people trying to make a living.

Brian pressed the door release. "Bugger off," he said.

The kid looked almost disappointed that Brian hadn't put up more of an argument. But after a moment's hesitation, he climbed out of the cab.

Adding insult to injury, when he was a few feet away, the teenager turned and flipped Brian the bird.

And that's what did it. That's what made Brian lose it.

He stamped on the accelerator, driving right for the little bastard.

Brian felt a warm glow of satisfaction when the kid turned, panic plastered all over his face.

The kid ran towards an alleyway. He obviously hoped to escape that way, but he was out of luck. The little alleyway was just wide enough for Brian's cab.

He sped after the kid. The brickwork on either side of the alleyway made an awful screeching noise as it scraped along the cab, but Brian paid no attention. He was focused solely on catching the kid.

He was almost on top of him, when the alleyway ended and they were back on a street. Brian didn't know which one and he didn't care. All he cared about was catching the little sod.

Later Brian would say, he didn't see the man at all. How could he? One moment, it was just Brian's cab and the runaway kid on the street. The next, some crazy guy was running towards him.

Brian had slammed on the brakes, but it was too late.

Two thousand kilos of metal ploughed into the man with a sickening crunch.

Mackinnon heard the sound of screeching rubber against tarmac, and he held his breath. Jesus. That hadn't sounded good.

They caught up with the wreck two streets away. A black cab stood in the middle of the road.

In front of it, Kwame Okoro lay on the pavement. Deep red blood oozed from a head wound.

The cab driver, a short man of around fifty, wearing a buttoned cardigan, had climbed out of the cab to inspect the damage.

His hands flew up to his mouth. "Oh, God. It wasn't my fault. He came out of nowhere."

"Ambulance is on its way," Collins said. "But I think he's past help."

Mackinnon kneeled beside Kwame Okoro's body and felt for a pulse. Nothing.

He shook his head at Collins.

Mackinnon could hear the distant wail of a siren. The ambulance might be too late for Kwame Okoro, but he hoped it wasn't too late for Lisa Stratton.

"Do we know what happened to the woman?" Mackinnon asked. "Lisa Stratton?"

One of the uniforms heard Mackinnon's question and stepped forward. "She's all right. He's cut her up a bit, but it looks like she'll pull through."

Mackinnon waited for the wave of relief to wash over him, but it didn't come.

This case was such a mess. Kwame Okoro might be dead, but how were they going to prove the case against all the others who had been involved?

Kwame had basically been acting as a hit man for hire. How would they get justice for Francis Eze, Adam Jonah and Mark Fleming?

Their enemies had signed their death warrants and it was starting to look like they would get away with it.

CHAPTER FORTY-THREE

MACKINNON'S JOURNEY BACK TO WOOD Street station was subdued.

Lisa Stratton had been rushed straight to hospital in an ambulance, and an hour later Tyler received feedback from the doctor in charge of Lisa Stratton's treatment. Thankfully her injuries were not life-threatening.

The cuts to her back were deep and would result in nasty scars. Hundreds of sutures had been needed to hold the wounds together. Later Lisa Stratton would need plastic surgery, too, in an effort to minimise scarring.

After they'd cracked an investigation, the team's mood was normally buoyant and lighthearted, but now everyone was sitting quietly at their own desks, trying to process what had happened.

Collins wandered up to Mackinnon's desk. He'd taken off his tie and stuffed it in his pocket.

"Do you fancy a drink after work?" he asked.

Mackinnon nodded. He could do with something to help him unwind. He was planning to stay at Derek's tonight, and Derek would be out on another date with Julie, the last thing Mackinnon wanted was to go home alone and brood.

Collins glanced at his watch. "Hell of a lot of paperwork," he said. "But I could be ready in an hour or so."

"Sounds good," Mackinnon said, then stared down at the pile of forms on his desk.

DC Webb wandered into the major incident room, cracking his fingers.

"I'll give Okoro credit for one thing," he said. "He made the paperwork easier. Shame all our criminals don't jump in front of taxis."

No one in the room looked up or reacted to DC Webb. Black humour often lightened the mood as a way of giving off steam, but in this case, it wasn't working.

And it wouldn't make the paperwork easier really. There'd be another investigation into Kwame Okoro's death, and one way or another it would end up being the police's fault.

Mackinnon looked across at Charlotte. She was sitting in front of her computer, with her hands raised to press the keys, but she wasn't actually doing anything. She was staring blankly at the screen.

DC Webb walked across to her desk and tapped her on the shoulder. "There's someone downstairs who wants to see you," he said.

Charlotte frowned. "Who?"

"The teacher from Poplar Comprehensive, Mr. Xander. He's got the boy with him, too."

Charlotte scrambled out of her chair.

"Alfie? They found him? Fantastic."

"Yes," DC Webb said. "And he wants to talk to you."

CHAPTER FORTY-FOUR

CHARLOTTE HURRIED DOWN THE STEPS. Her heart was pounding.

Thank God. Thank God. Thank God.

The words kept running through her head.

Alfie Adebayo's aunt had been charged, but his Uncle Remi was still missing. Charlotte had feared he'd taken the boy off somewhere.

She got to the front desk, and the duty sergeant, Frank Dobson, tilted his head. "They're waiting for you," he said.

Mr. William Xander and Alfie were sitting in the orange plastic chairs in reception.

When he saw her, Mr. Xander stood up. His huge frame dwarfed the chair he'd been sitting in and he towered over Alfie and Charlotte.

Alfie stood up beside him. He'd taken his coat off, and for the first time, Charlotte noticed just how skinny his arms and legs were. Was he malnourished? Or was he in the middle of a growth spurt? She hoped it was the latter.

Alfie's skinny arms and legs just made Mr. Xander look even bigger.

The teacher put a meaty hand on Alfie's shoulder.

"He's come to talk to you," he said. "He wants to tell you everything that has happened."

Charlotte looked at Alfie, but he wouldn't meet her gaze. He was chewing his lip and looking down at his shoes.

"That's great," Charlotte said. "But because he is a minor, we will have to organise a special interview."

Mr. Xander put a hand up and took two steps toward Charlotte.

"I know there is a procedure," he said in a low voice as he leaned close to her ear. "But he wants to talk now, and he wants to talk to you."

"Me specifically?" Charlotte asked.

"Yeah. He said he wanted to talk to Charlotte, the short police officer with the dark hair."

Charlotte took another look at Alfie who was looking even more uncomfortable.

She nodded. "All right."

She turned to face the desk and told Frank they'd be using the family room.

"We'll be more comfortable in here," she said, leading the way along the corridor and then opening the door to the family room.

Inside, she gestured for them both to sit down on the comfy, bright-green sofas.

"I have to say," Charlotte began. "That none of this is going to be recorded. This is just a chat. Okay, Alfie?"

Alfie looked terrified, but he managed to nod.

Charlotte thought she should start by explaining to the boy what had happened to his aunt.

His aunt may have been partly responsible for the death of Alfie's friend, Francis, and many others, but most abused children didn't stop loving their family because they treated them badly.

"Your aunt has been charged," Charlotte said carefully. "There'll be a trial, and this won't be over very quickly."

There was no point sugarcoating the truth. At twelve-years old, Alfie was old enough to hear this.

Alfie nodded.

"Tell her about the baths, Alfie," Mr. Xander said, putting his large hand on the boy's shoulder.

Alfie rested his forearms on his knees, staring down at the ground. He began to speak in a very quiet voice.

He told her about the ablutions and the exorcism to get rid of the evil that lived within him. He described how they used to try and wash the spirit away by submerging him underwater until he was gasping, desperate to take a breath.

Charlotte listened in horror to the abuse this boy had suffered.

Mr. Xander gave the boy's shoulder another squeeze.

"Carry on Alfie," he said. "Tell her about the people who came to the flat to ask your aunt for Mr. X's help."

Charlotte held her breath. They'd been expecting this. Alfie would be a key witness. If he had seen Joy Barter and the others meeting with his aunt, this could be the evidence they needed. At the same time, for Alfie's sake, she wished he hadn't seen them. The next few months could be hell for the boy.

Alfie's voice trembled as he described the people who had come to his aunt for help.

"Thank you, Alfie," Charlotte said. "I know this isn't easy."

Later when Alfie was officially interviewed, they would show him photographs of all the suspects and let him identify them.

"There's more," Mr. Xander said, turning his intense brown eyes onto Alfie.

Alfie blinked a couple of times, looked up at Mr. Xander then took a deep breath.

Charlotte thought she'd have to remind the teacher not to interrupt or prompt the boy if he was present when they did the official interview.

But his presence did seem to reassure Alfie.

There were officers who had special training for dealing with minors. They went on courses and learned how to talk about things like this. They learned the right questions to ask, without making the child feel pressured. But Charlotte hadn't taken any of those courses. She felt desperately out of her depth.

Charlotte leaned forward.

"It's all right, Alfie," she said. "If you want to stop here, that's okay,"

Alfie bit down on his lip and shook his head, then he looked up.

His deep brown eyes fixed on Charlotte and he said, "I know why he killed Francis."

"We saw a murder."

Back in the incident room, Mackinnon picked up his mobile phone. There were still piles of paperwork to get through, but he'd almost finished writing up his account of what had happened that afternoon.

But there was something else preying on his mind. He was worried about Katy. He decided to go outside, take a breath of fresh air and give Chloe a call to see how they were getting on.

He hoped Chloe would tell him that it had been something and nothing, and the children had buried the hatchet. Kids argued all the time. It might not be as serious as Mackinnon thought.

But when Chloe answered the phone, Mackinnon could tell straight away that the situation hadn't resolved itself.

"I'm at my wits' end, Jack," she said. "Katy's refusing to go back to school now. I really think she's scared of them."

It was funny how you could live with someone and never notice something was wrong.

He'd heard of kids a bit older than Katy committing suicide because of bullying and their parents had been totally unaware anything was the matter.

Mackinnon had always found that hard to accept before. How could you not notice?

"I'm really worried about her, Jack," Chloe said.

Mackinnon walked a little further away from the station entrance. His breath produced white clouds as he exhaled.

He looked out at the squad cars in the car park. "Have you spoken to anyone at the school?" he asked.

He heard Chloe sigh on the other end of the line. "Yes, I've made an appointment for tomorrow to see the headmaster and Katy's head of year. Do you think I should make her go back to school tomorrow?"

Mackinnon put his hand against the rough brick exterior wall, propping himself up. He suddenly felt bone weary.

"A day off won't make a difference," he said. "It might help. Maybe you could keep her off school until you've spoken to the headmaster."

Chloe hesitated, then said, "You're probably right, but what if she refuses to ever go back to school?"

"There are other schools," Mackinnon said.

"Not as good as this one. It could ruin her future."

So could being bullied for the next three years, Mackinnon thought.

CHAPTER FORTY-FIVE

INSIDE THE FAMILY ROOM, CHARLOTTE tucked her hands under her knees so Alfie couldn't see that her hands were shaking.

"A murder, Alfie? Whose murder did you see?"

Alfie shook his head. "I don't know who it was. We saw a man on the floor, and I saw Mr. X above him. He had a knife in his hand… and he stabbed him."

Alfie's lashes were wet with tears.

"It was just me and Francis. Francis told me he knew who Mr. X was, and said he could show me where he lived. I didn't believe him. I thought Mr. X was just someone my aunt and uncle made up to scare me."

Alfie chewed his thumbnail. "I should have believed Francis," he said. "Then we might not have seen it.

"I knew there was something wrong, and I wanted to run away, but Francis didn't… He just stood there, and then..." Alfie broke off and put a hand to his mouth. He shook his head and then said, "I ran away."

A tear rolled down his cheek. "I ran away and left Francis there."

Charlotte swallowed the lump in her throat. "I'm glad you ran away, Alfie. That was the sensible thing to do."

"But if I hadn't run away, maybe Francis..."

"No boy," Mr. Xander's low voice rumbled. "If you hadn't run away... it doesn't bear thinking about. You staying wouldn't have saved Francis."

"You did the right thing," Charlotte said again. "And now you're really helping Francis by telling us all this."

Alfie had witnessed a murder. His best friend had been killed and dumped in a river. He'd been abused by his aunt and uncle, and abandoned by his grandmother.

Despite all that, when Alfie looked at Charlotte, he didn't look nervous any more, he looked relieved.

When Charlotte walked back to the incident room, she felt more drained than she'd thought possible.

Alfie would be staying with emergency foster carers overnight. He had to be so scared. He was only twelve-years-old and he'd been through so much. Now that he was a witness, he'd have to live through it all again when they had a trial.

As she walked along the corridor, she saw Mackinnon, Collins and Webb heading out of the incident room.

"Drink?" Mackinnon asked.

Charlotte nodded. After today, she needed more than one.

· · ·

Inside the Red Herring Pub, Charlotte looked up at the plastic spiders hanging from the ceiling.

There were spray-on cobwebs at the window. Hollowed-out pumpkins with candles inside sat on the windowsills and gave out an eerie flickering light.

This was one Halloween Charlotte would never forget.

Charlotte's phone buzzed in her pocket, and she pulled it out, smiling when she saw who the message was from.

Last year she'd bought Nan a mobile phone, but Nan hadn't warmed to it straight away. It had been months before she'd attempted a text, but now she was in full swing and sent Charlotte a text practically every day.

Charlotte read the text and quickly replied. She'd go and see Nan tomorrow. Charlotte had needed to bail out on their weekly dinner last Wednesday, and she'd felt bad.

Charlotte smothered a yawn and added an order of chicken wings to Mackinnon and Collins's food order. The bruise was now blossoming on the side of Mackinnon's head. It would look awful in the morning.

She watched the condensation trickle down the side of her gin and tonic and thought about how things could have worked out differently.

She thought about the piece of paper Erika Darago had pushed towards her and how tempted she'd been to write down a name.

They now had months of work in front of them as they tried to get justice for Kofi Okoro's victims. Every murder had been paid for but proving that would be hard. The cases against Joy Barter, Eric Madison and Bertie Lassiter needed to be watertight; otherwise they would walk.

So many lives had been wrecked. At least Alfie Adebayo had been taken away from his abusive family and was now in emergency foster care. Charlotte hoped Alfie could get the help and support he needed, so his life wasn't ruined as well.

If anyone deserved some happiness, it was him.

CHAPTER FORTY-SIX

TWO MONTHS LATER, CHARLOTTE TRUDGED over a muddy playing field. There were only a few days until Christmas, and Charlotte thought whoever had decided a football match was a good idea at this time of year was crazy.

She wasn't exactly a football fan, but she'd been invited today by William Xander.

She spotted the PE teacher straight away. He stood head and shoulders above everyone else standing on the sidelines.

He waved her over.

Charlotte wrapped her scarf more securely around her neck and joined him at the edge of the pitch.

"Who's winning?" she asked.

William Xander laughed. "It's just a kick about," he said, and nodded at Alfie who was dribbling the ball. "He's good though. The boy has a real talent."

"He looks a lot smaller than the other boys," Charlotte said as Alfie successfully skirted around a tackle from a boy almost a foot taller than him.

"That's because most of them are fifteen. But he holds his own."

Charlotte really wasn't much of a judge. She watched them play for a few minutes then said, "How has he been getting on?"

"Pretty good. I think he worries about his uncle, but he's getting better."

Alfie's uncle, Remi Darago, had disappeared without a trace. Charlotte knew that until the man was found and held accountable, Alfie would find it hard to focus on the future.

"Do you think the football helps?" Charlotte asked.

"It helps him to know he is good at something. Last month, I asked him to try out for the school team and he told me he was terrible at sports. That's what he's been told his whole life, so he believes it."

William Xander shouted out, "Keep your eyes on the ball, Alfie."

"Is he doing okay at school?"

Xander nodded. "Yes, which is largely thanks to his foster placement. He got lucky there." Xander nodded further along the sidelines where a group of parents gathered. "His foster mother is here. Shall I introduce you?"

Alfie's foster mother was a short woman, almost as short as Charlotte. She had a sunny smile and greeted Charlotte enthusiastically when Xander introduced them.

Xander blew his whistle. "All right, you lot. That's enough for today."

Along with the other boys, Alfie trudged off the pitch. He was smiling. He really looked happy.

He was heading over towards his foster mother when he saw Charlotte and froze.

The fear on his face was obvious.

She shouldn't have come. She should have realised that her presence would just remind Alfie of everything he'd been through, and the trial he still had to endure.

"Come on, boy," Mr. Xander's voice boomed. "She's just come to see if you're okay. There's nothing to worry about.

Alfie nodded and took a tentative step forward. His foster mother walked over to him and ruffled his hair. "You did great today. Absolutely brilliant."

Alfie smiled and took a juice from Mr. Xander. He guzzled it down greedily.

"You played well, Alfie," Charlotte said.

"Thanks," he said shyly.

She chatted with him for a few minutes, and he enthusiastically described his new house and the new football boots he'd had for his birthday. It was nice to hear him talk about things kids his age *should* be talking about. And it was fantastic to see how relaxed he was.

As they walked back to the school car park, Alfie and his foster mother walked slightly ahead of Charlotte and Mr. Xander.

Mr. Xander clamped a large hand on Charlotte's shoulder. "You know, I think he's going to be okay."

Charlotte smiled. In front of them, Alfie was discussing plans for Christmas with his foster mother.

"I think you're right," she said.

There was still a long way to go, but Alfie was definitely heading in the right direction.

THANK YOU!

THANKS FOR READING DEADLY RITUAL. I hope you enjoyed it!

I am currently working on the next book in the Deadly Series. If you would like to be one of the first to find out when my next book is available, you can sign up for my new release email at www.dsbutlerbooks.com/newsletter

Reviews are like gold to authors. They spread the word and help readers find books, and I appreciate all reviews whether positive or negative. If you have the time to leave a review, I would be very grateful.

You can follow me on Twitter at @ds_butler, or like my Facebook page at http://facebook.com/d.s.butler.author

If you would like to read a short extract of Deadly Payback, please turn the page.

EXTRACT FROM DEADLY PAYBACK

AT FOURTEEN, I WOULD NEVER have believed I would become a killer.

People think that killers are different somehow, missing that vital component that tells the rest of the population the difference between right and wrong. But that's not true. Up until I was fourteen, I was perfectly normal. Even now, I wasn't what people would expect from a killer.

I don't torture animals. I have a steady job. I love my mother. I like to watch soaps on TV. I'm just like everyone else, except for one thing: I am about to commit murder.

I could still back out, turn around and go home, but even though that thought was there at the back of my mind, I didn't consider it seriously. I'd been waiting for this moment for years. Obsessing, daydreaming, plotting... It had taken over my life.

There was no going back now.

The view from the fifty-second floor of the Shard was

breathtaking. The City of London spread out before me, and I could see the snaking outline of the Thames. I stared at the lights reflected on the river's surface, unable to wrench my eyes away. For a moment, the murmur of voices in the bar seemed to melt into the background as I drank in the view. I'd never seen London from this viewpoint before. It was beautiful.

A voice behind me cut through my thoughts, and I turned around.

I smiled at the barman and reached out a shaky hand to grasp the stem of my champagne glass. I paid him and waited for my change.

I glanced to my left and right, making sure I hadn't attracted any unwanted attention. Sipping on my drink, I tried to relax and fit in. I needed to act normally tonight. Everything depended on it.

I smiled at the barman as he pushed my change towards me, but he barely glanced at me before he moved on to serve the man to my right. And that was a good thing — it was exactly what I wanted.

I surveyed the room. It was busy, but no one was paying attention to me. I grabbed my coat and carried my glass over to a table where I could sit with a view of the entrance.

A loud laugh from a group over by the floor-to-ceiling windows made me jump. They looked like an office group, having an early Christmas party. One of the men wore a Santa hat. I wouldn't have thought that this was the type of place to hold a Christmas party. I guessed they had to be bankers. Or perhaps they worked in insurance. It had to be a job which paid them an obscene amount of money. The cost of drinks here was extortionate.

I looked away and sat down.

She wasn't here yet. I could feel the swell of panic building in my chest. I forced myself to calm down, and took another sip of my champagne, savouring the sensation of bubbles on my tongue. But then I put the glass back on the table. I couldn't drink too much. I needed to keep my wits about me tonight.

Two women drifted past my table, their faces plastered with a ridiculous amount of makeup. I wrinkled my nose at the strong, cloying scent one of them wore. It smelled like cheap air freshener.

I checked my watch. The reception party should be over by now. I'd been so sure she'd come here for a drink afterwards. My whole plan rested on her habits. But it was risky. She might not come to the bar at all. Maybe she'd gone straight back to her room and ordered a drink from room service.

I clenched my fists on my lap. It didn't matter. Either way, she wouldn't escape.

A movement to my right caught my attention, and I inhaled sharply when I saw her.

She wasn't alone. She was with a friend — a man.

I narrowed my eyes as I watched them, glad that the bar was dark and I could sit there unnoticed.

Beverley Madison was petite, blonde and successful. Anyone sitting within ten feet of her would know that because she was taking great delight in loudly telling her male companion just how she had amazed everyone in the industry by creating a bidding war for her client's new book at the book fair today.

To his credit, the man she was talking to didn't yawn once.

I hadn't been wrong about her drinking. As they chatted, she guzzled down three glasses of champagne. Her companion was still on his first drink.

When she finally drained her third glass, she got up, unsteady on her feet. She scooped up her bag, kissed her friend on both cheeks and headed out of the bar.

I almost smiled in relief when I realised he wasn't going with her. That would definitely make things easier for me.

I wanted to follow her straight away, and it took all my willpower to stay seated at my table by the exit. My hands gripped the edge of the smooth polished wood as I tried to focus my attention on her friend, who remained in the bar. He ordered another drink and asked for his bill.

It was almost time.

I knew from my research the man's name was Barry Henderson. He was a work colleague and had known Beverley for years. He checked his mobile phone, scrolling through the screen.

The minutes passed slowly.

Hurry up, you stupid man. Finish your drink.

Finally, he stood up, dropping a bank note on the table for a tip. As he started to make his way out of the bar, he dialled a number on his mobile phone.

Grabbing my stuff, I followed him. I slipped my arms in the sleeves of my heavy coat and raised the hood.

With my face hidden to the CCTV camera, I smiled as I

entered the lift. Barry Henderson still had his phone clamped to his ear and was paying me no attention.

He pushed his hotel key card into the slot and pressed the button for the forty-fourth floor.

He glanced at me then, with a questioning look.

"I need the forty-fourth floor, too," I said and smiled again.

It wasn't an act. It was a genuine smile. Barry Henderson might not realise it yet, but he was helping me. Beverley Madison was about to meet her maker, and I couldn't be happier.

DEADLY PAYBACK is available now.

ACKNOWLEDGMENTS

MANY PEOPLE HELPED TO PROVIDE ideas and background for this book. My thanks and gratitude to DI Dave Carter for his help when I first had the idea for the Deadly Series.

To Nanci, my editor, thanks for always managing to squeeze me in when I finally finish my books!

I would also like to thank my friends on Twitter for their entertaining tweets and encouragement.

My thanks, too, to all the people who read the story and gave helpful suggestions and to Chris, who, as always, supported me despite the odds.

And last but not least, my thanks to you for reading this book. I hope you enjoyed it.

Printed in Great Britain
by Amazon

41799764R00170